Telescopin

The Earlywor
Science Fiction Cl

set by and dedicated to

David Dennis

Earlyworks Press

Telescoping Time

Copyright Information

Cover image: Doug McGuffey standing next to the Integrated Science Instrument Module (ISIM) Flight Structure. Photo courtesy of NASA/GSFC/Chris Gunn

Paperback ISBN 978-1-906451-56-1

Ebook ISBN 978-1-906451-57-8

Printed in the UK
By MPG Book Group

Published by Earlyworks Press
Creative Media Centre,
45 Robertson St, Hastings,
Sussex TN34 1HL

www.earlyworkspress.co.uk

Contents

Last Contact	by R. J. Allison	1
The Cover Story	by Brindley Hallam Dennis	7
In Their Image	by Rosemary Goodacre	11
Stars in the Water	by Andrea Tang	18
How Do You Feel	by Robert Leonard	23
Protocol 909	by Peter Rolls	31
Searching for P'tach	by Andrew Irvine	41
The Decision	by Chris Sanderson	46
Haze	by K S Dearsley	52

About Earlyworks Press Genre Challenges 64

Last Contact

by R. J. Allison

Everybody remembers where they were when the Message stopped. We'd been expecting it, of course. The first section decoded, the header, had clearly specified the length of the whole transmission. The Message had been streaming in for decades, but we knew exactly when it would come to an end. Ceremonies had been planned across the world to commemorate the moment, but that moment never arrived. The Message just stopped, suddenly, abruptly, and several months too soon.

'The Silencers have got them,' said Prentiss. 'That's what they get for giving away their position.'

He and I, and seventeen other people, were on board the UN Research Vessel *Relayer*, orbiting Neptune. I was running some tests on the transmitter array when the news came over the ship's PA system. Prentiss sat beside me in the engineering module, checking the secondary power system. His comment broke the moment of startled silence which followed the announcement.

'The Silencers are just a legend,' I said, as much for my benefit as his. Cool reason would restore our courage. 'Transmission could fail for any number of technical reasons. Or natural ones.'

He said nothing but I could tell he wasn't convinced. I looked at the schematic of the transmitter array on the screen, and a tingle of alarm passed through me. What if he was right?

As I made my way from the engineering module to accommodation module 2, I felt the floor sway and vibrate slightly under my feet. Those tiny intermittent movements occurred all over the ship – as the gravity management system trimmed ballast, tuned rotation speed, and generally stabilised the rotationally-induced artificial gravity – but on the tubeways between the modules they were always stronger. I imagined them as the spacefarer's equivalent of the swell of the sea and the thrum of engines through the deck of a ship on an Earthly ocean.

I could have no illusions about where I really was, though. The tubeway walls were transparent plastic and through them I could see the slowly rotating starscape beyond the ship, and the huge blue-green crescent of Neptune with his attendant moons. I could also see the transmitter array, following its own orbit close to ours. We had towed the huge structure all the way from Earth, but it would remain here long years after we had departed. Whether or not it would actually do anything remained to be decided.

I entered the common room of the accommodation module and sat down near two of the people who would make that decision. Krishnamurti and Paxton were the only others in the room and were too caught up in their own conversation to acknowledge my arrival. I was used to this, and I accepted it. The members of the Jury had a great responsibility and I had no wish to distract them from that. The Jury's discussions were open, and would form part of the historical record, but I liked the idea of being the first to hear them, well before the communication laser could beam their words across the light-hours to Earth.

'Do we really want to be part of the Silence?' said Krishnamurti. The Silence is that part of the galaxy which never returns transmissions, or whose transmissions have unaccountably stopped. Hence the myth of the Silencers – a scary explanation for the fact of the Silence. Many civilisations across the galaxy have such myths, but there's no direct evidence that hostile super-beings really do track down transmitting worlds and destroy them. Most people think the Silencers don't really exist. Or maybe we just hope that.

'If we send out the Message and the Silencers home in on our beam, we certainly will be part of the Silence,' said Paxton.

I thought Krishnamurti would pour scorn on what he would call her superstition, but he surprised me with his reply.

'If we send out the Message, it doesn't matter if the Silencers get us – or solar flares, or whatever,' said Krishnamurti. 'Our legacy will be out there, part of the Message, going on to new peoples forever. Even if our civilisation dies, its spirit will last for ever.'

The Message contains layer upon layer, like an archaeological site; every re-transmitting civilisation adds its own contribution to the ever-growing mass of material. It's a gigantic chain letter, millions of years old. Much of the material is obscure, hard to decode, hard to understand (especially where it derives from life-forms radically different from us). Much of the Message has been sent on by the Transmitters without them having decoded or understood it. In fact they have explicitly requested us to send them anything new we glean from those layers of the Message. Of course, they've added their own layer, just as we will add ours, if we decide to Transmit.

The Message holds more than information or knowledge. Some of it is binary code for autonomous advanced programs – artificial intelligences, avatars of distant or long-extinct aliens. Bartu, the ambassador of the Transmitters, is one of those; he's hosted on a giant mainframe at UN headquarters. Some of the Message consists of DNA sequences which code for physical organisms. When our biotechnology improves sufficiently, we'll be able to recreate those organisms. One day, we'll have aliens as a physical presence right here on Earth. Bartu will undulate into the Council Chamber itself, to present his credentials in person to the assembled Sample of All Humanity.

'There has been no original research on Earth since the Message began,' countered Paxton. 'All our thoughts have been bent to extracting its meaning. Do we really want to pass on that stifling legacy?'

'We owe it to the Transmitters,' said Krishnamurti. 'Think of all the benefits we've had from the Message. They've asked us to pass it on. We owe them that.'

The Message had already changed human society for ever, by revealing the secret of good government. If you want fair, wise, representative government – just take random samples of the population, give them free access to information, and let them make the decisions. We should have realised earlier, of course. We'd been using the secret in a limited way for centuries, in the courts. It took the Message to reveal that's how all advanced civilisations run their affairs, and to put the Universal Jury Principle at the centre of our political life. Tyranny and elitism, the intrigues of party politics, the cumbersome unreliable machinery of elections – all swept away. Now we would use that same principle to decide whether or not to send on the Message to others.

Paxton opened her mouth, but I never learned what she made of Krishnamurti's remark, for the floor's faint vibration turned suddenly into a sharp, sickening heave that threw me out of my seat. Coffee cups skidded across the table where the others sat, and Paxton pitched forward across it.

'Emergency!' barked Captain Hart over the PA system. 'All hands to in-flight manouevre stations. All passengers don safety harnesses. This is an emergency.'

The heaving and jerking of the module continued as Krishnamurti and Paxton scrambled to the safety harnesses on one wall and buckled themselves in; I was grateful that they had remembered the drills we did on the journey out. I half-climbed, half-fell down the vertical access ladder into the module's control cubicle. My hands flashed over the controls and Captain Hart's face appeared on screen.

'Richards!' he said. 'Good. I had to fire up the manouevring motors. The transmitter array changed orbit, it was on a collision course.' He glanced to the side, checking a display I couldn't see. 'We're all right now, the gravity system should stabilise soon.'

I nodded – the juddering of the floor was less already.

'Krishnamurti and Paxton are safely buckled in,' I said.

'Good,' he replied, glancing again at the off-screen display. 'That accounts for everybody, except Prentiss. Have you any idea where he is?'

Cold fear clutched at me. Suddenly I knew exactly where Prentiss was.

The giant spider web of the transmitter array loomed ahead of me, dominating the view through my suit's faceplate. Slowly it grew larger, as I drifted closer, homing in on the control module at the centre. Behind me, I knew, floated the complex honeycomb of struts and modules that was the *Relayer*. I imagined myself as a tiny dot drifting between the two giant artefacts, themselves floating in the vastness of space; it was not a comforting thought.

It had not taken long to confirm my sudden intuition about Prentiss. The control link from *Relayer* to the transmitter array had been cut off manually, from the array's control module. Prentiss had changed the array's orbit from in there; now he and it were on a course that would plunge into the atmosphere of Neptune, destroying the array.

'But he'll be killed too!' I'd said when the Captain confirmed the new trajectory.

‘I don’t think he cares,’ said the Captain. ‘You heard him when we tried to make contact.’ Prentiss had raved briefly about the Silencers and then cut off the comms link. He was clearly beyond reason.

The control module filled the view now, and I manoeuvred the suit towards the airlock. We had several hours before the trajectories of the ship and the array would diverge too far for suits to travel between them. That was our window of opportunity to take back control and save the array. And Prentiss.

I clunked against the airlock door and its automatic cycle began. At least Prentiss hadn’t sabotaged that. A few minutes later I was inside the airlock, sliding out of my suit as I floated in zero-gee at the centre of the chamber. A curving access tube led towards the control room at the heart of the module. I drifted along it cautiously, one hand on the wall, one clutching the sedative hypo intended for Prentiss. A final curve, and I emerged into the control chamber.

Banks of displays and controls covered all the walls and what would have been floor and ceiling in the presence of gravity. Prentiss floated in the middle, curled up into a foetal ball. His eyes opened and he looked wearily at me.

‘Richards,’ he whispered.

‘Don’t worry,’ I said, smiling, drifting closer. ‘It’s going to be all right.’ If I could just get to him before he did anything crazy…

‘What if they come?’ he said. ‘The Silencers – what if they come?’ He was trembling with fear. In a way I didn’t blame him. The Message contains some disturbing material; most civilisations have dark blots on their history, and there has been evil among the stars as there has on Earth. I’d read transcripts from the last days of Ardavil, the annihilation of Gempar, the transmutation of Iladon – they kept me awake some nights too. And no doubt other beings will quail at our accounts of Auschwitz and Hiroshima. But that’s not the whole story. The universe is big, and some of it is scary, but a lot of it is kind, and wise, and just brilliant. Like life, really, only more so.

‘It isn’t up to us,’ I said. ‘We’re crew. The hard choice has to be made by our passengers, the Jury.’ I was close enough to touch him now. I reached out and took his shuddering form in my arms, gathered him to me like a little child. ‘It’s all right. I’ve got you.’

Prentiss was still in sickbay under sedation when the moment of decision came. Captain Hart and I had sealed the members of the Jury in their individual cabins; they would not emerge until the issue was decided. I was with the Captain on *Relayer*'s bridge. The control panel showed all members of the Jury logged in to the main computer. Their decision would directly control the transmitter array. Each Juror controlled a switch; if they were all turned on, the transmitter would be activated. A single 'no' would prevent Transmission.

I had no idea how they would vote; nor, I guessed, did most of them. I've been on various juries myself, of course, and I know there are times when you're sure early on, but there are others when you don't know how you'll vote until you do. Sometimes it's as much a matter of discovery as of decision. Surely this was one of those.

A gentle chime from the computer announced the votes were in. I looked at the control panel. The transmitter array was active; the Jury had decided – we would not be part of the Silence.

We had joined the Conversation.

The Cover Story

by Brindley Hallam Dennis

Two men in badly fitting suits came into the bar and walked over to my table. They said, are you the writer?

I said, I'm a writer.

They said, you wrote a story called The Cover Story?

I said, that's right.

They said, that's a strange story.

I said, it's science fiction.

Is that a fact? the big one said.

I said, I wrote it for a competition.

Now where did you get an idea like that from? the little one asked.

I said, where do any ideas come from? And he looked at the big one.

Where indeed, the big one said, and they both looked at me.

I said, what's this all about?

Refresh my memory, the big one said, about the story, and he added, go get us a drink Jake, and the little one went off to the bar. The big one leaned in close. Don't worry too much about my partner, he said, if he seems a little over eager.

Over eager about what? I asked.

About your story, he said.

I said, where did you hear about it?

He said, you said it was in a competition.

I said, yes, but it didn't win. I said, have you read it?

He said, oh, yes. We've read it all right, and then the little one came back with three drinks on a small round tray, which he set down awkwardly on the table.

The barman says this is what you drink, he said, lifting off the glasses. He pushed them one by one towards us, like three points of a triangle. Then he put the tray on its edge, leaning against one of the legs of the table. Tell us about it, he said, the story.

I didn't know what he was getting at. I said, what about it?

The big one said, just give us the bare bones. It's about some spacemen, right?

A party of astronauts, I said, sort of.

Sort of? the little one said, looking puzzled.

Well, I said, it's not clear, at first, who they are.

No? the big one said.

I said, they've come back.

He said, the astronauts?

I said, yes. They've come back in a comet.

A comet? the little one said.

You know about comets? the big one asked.

Of course I know about comets, I said. Everyone knows about comets.

Enough to write a story? the big one asked.

Enough to write this story, I said. All you have to know is that they get frozen and then thaw out again when they pass the sun, that and the fact that it's a hell of a long time before they come back again. They each took a drink then, and I said, look, what's all this about?

They said, it's about your story, The Cover Story. They said, that's about these guys, right, who get sent up and are frozen into a comet going around the sun. Have I got that right? the big one asked.

Yes, more or less, I said,

And then they come back to this planet? the little one asked.

But nobody knows they've been sent up in the first place, the big one said.

I said, that's the twist in the tail.

The tail of the comet? the little one asked.

No, the big one said, giving him a look, the tail of the story.

I said, it's a Cold War story.

The Cold War's been over a long time, the big one said.

I said, I know.

He said, people don't want to read about stuff that happened so long ago.

I said, but it's set in the future, when the war's over and forgotten.

Oh yeah! The big one said, and he nodded as if that had just occurred to him. I can see that now, he said.

I said, you're supposed to think that when they come back they aren't who we think they are.

Who do we think they are? the little one asked.

We don't know who they are, I said. It's who the people in the story think they are that matters, I said. I said, because there's no record of them having been sent in the first place.

Neither of them said anything then.

I said, but what you don't know is whether or not they really were sent, and you don't know if that's because of them being sent and the records were destroyed, or because they were sent by someone else or even that they weren't sent but have come from somewhere else, and are only pretending to be who they seem to be.

That's a lot of stuff we don't know, said the big one, but the little one tapped him on the arm and said, over eagerly, what do you mean pretending?

Well, I explained, they might not actually be pretending, so much as believing it themselves.

That's some story, the big one said.

Thank you, I told him.

He said, and these records, who could have destroyed them, and why?

I said, the enemy. I said, an enemy spy, a mole, Burgess and MacClean. I said, that sort of thing was going on all the time in those days.

So why would this Burgess Maclean want to do something like that, the little one asked?

Them, I said, there were two of them, maybe more. I said, he would have done it to discredit them, if they were really who they said they were, so that they wouldn't be believed.

That's a very interesting theory, the little one said.

Thanks, I said, but it wasn't interesting enough to win the competition. I said, it didn't even get into the long list.

You win some, the big one said, and pulled a face.

Why did you pick that particular comet, the little one asked?

I said, I thought it seemed to come around about right.

About right? The little one asked.

For the time they would have had to be sent up, and for when they would be coming back, I said.

The big one didn't look convinced. Cryogenics was big back then, I told him, and people thought that the Cold War would go on for ever, or end in a nuclear war.

And no-one knows who they are, your astronauts? the little one persisted

No, not for sure, I said.

Nor where they've really come from, the big one said.

Unless somebody did know, but was keeping quiet about it? the little one said, and he looked enquiringly at the big one.

Nobody knows, I said.

In your story, the big one said.

Of course, in my story.

If nobody knew, the big one said, there would be no story.

They'd still arrive, I said. People would know that. That would be the story.

Some people would know, the little one said, nodding.

The right people, the big one said, and he nodded too.

I don't know what you're getting at, I told them. I hadn't touched my beer, but I suddenly felt that I needed a drink.

The problem is always what to do about the people who do know, the big one said.

But who shouldn't, the little one added.

That's not what the story is about, I said.

No, the big one said. Your story's not about that at all.

The two of them finished their drinks and got up to leave.

You're not thinking of sending that story to any other competitions are you? the big one asked.

No, I lied.

I think that's very wise, the little one said, and then they both left the bar, and I realised that I still didn't know where they'd read the story, and then my foot, which was trembling a little, must have caught the tray, leaning up against the table-leg, because suddenly it rolled out into the centre of the floor and fell, spinning like a tossed coin, noisy as a dustbin lid, flattening out with the sound of metal fantails on a snare drum.

In Their Image

by Rosemary Goodacre

'I told you they were androids,' Carlo insisted as he lounged with Peter and Jan in the rays of the warm Xenobian sun.

'They seem so intelligent,' Peter said: it was as though each had his own personality. 'Besides, what about the Message?'

'You know that was transmitted over a century ago,' Jan reminded him.

He sighed. Now they had seen an android being recharged he could no longer imagine they were alive. They had also seen the Warehouse, where broken down androids were recycled and new ones assembled from a complicated array of components, apparently made from electrical circuitry, metals and advanced kinds of plastic. The more he discovered about their structure the more he marvelled that the completed androids had limbs which moved as smoothly as those of live creatures, and features whose arrangements bore an uncanny resemblance to a human face.

'I'm off to compile our report,' said Carlo.

'Mind what you type out,' Peter begged. 'Don't make it sound – well, patronising, when you describe how they're built.'

Carlo stared at him. 'Why the hell should it matter, so long as my report's accurate?'

'It's just that Xweft and a few of the others are fluent in English: I'd hate them to be, er, offended….'

'I don't believe this. We've just proved they're machines – sophisticated, highly programmed, sure, but androids none the less!' He shrugged and set off for the Landing Area where most of their equipment was still kept. They could not transmit messages to Earth, much less hold a conversation, because of the immense time lapse. Their typed reports were sent off at least every two days in special communication pods which travelled the space between Xenobia and Earth even faster than their manned ship had done.

Peter recalled the moment on Earth three years earlier when their tracking station had received the message pulsed from the distant planet Xenobia. It had conformed to a coding convention in which the first two pulses suggested two numbers. When a grid of those dimensions was prepared the remainder of the Message fitted in, showing a distinct pattern: an artistic representation of a biped. Scientists and newsmen had flocked to the tracking station to wonder at the diagram from outer space. The life-form was elongated, and had extra fingers and strangely bulbous eyes, but its other features had been remarkably like those of a human.

At last they had an address, a distinct point in the universe from which intelligent beings were trying to contact them. It had taken only five years to raise the funds for the exploratory trip to Xenobia.

Luke, who co-ordinated the mission for Ground Control, had warned them to prepare for any eventuality. 'The Message took over a century to reach us,' he reminded them. 'Too bad they didn't have our latest technology for high-speed transmission.' The 2030's had brought this advance. 'Anything could have happened on the planet since then. The present rulers could be hostile.'

Now that spaceships could travel many times faster than the speed of light it had taken them only seven months to reach their destination. As they entered the atmosphere of the brown and blue planet the tedium of the voyage had been dispelled. Then, a few hours later, they had caught sight of an area of the surface where the usual brownish vegetation gave way to a vast area of scorched and pitted wasteland.

'They've had a nuclear war!' Jan cried in dismay. 'What else could cause devastation on that scale?'

'The Message must have been a distress call,' said Carlo.

Suppose they were too late, Peter thought desperately. 'We should still land,' he said. 'There may be survivors.'

They had circled a few more times and observed structures which looked like cities. They had made a cautious descent to a flat area near one of the cities. Their instruments outside the ship indicated a level of radiation which was high but not immediately dangerous to human life. By the time they slid back the hatch and stepped out on to Xenobia the first lanky creatures were approaching the ship, apparently as curious as they were.

Peter had stared: were these the beings who had sent the Message? Physically they matched the image of the tall bipeds with extra fingers and protruding eyes. The leading creature halted a little distance away and extended his arms towards them in a gesture of – what? Welcome? At least they did not look hostile. Peter stepped forward and clasped the hand of the creature in an approximation of a human handshake. 'We come in peace,' he uttered. The hand felt cold. 'We are from planet Earth, one hundred and twenty light years distant,' he added hesitantly. If his opposite number measured in light years his would probably be a different length.

The creature's large eyes glazed as though complicated thought processes were taking place. At last it gave a gurgle and began to articulate deep sounds almost like speech. 'From distant planet,' it repeated somewhat indistinctly. 'Peace.'

Peter exchanged glances with his colleagues. It had managed to repeat some of his words, almost as though it understood them. It gurgled again. 'Xweft,' it pronounced huskily, pointing to itself and initiating the first interplanetary introduction.

Xweft had been their first and most important contact on Xenobia. As they had become acclimatised they had noticed that each Xenobian had his own appointed task, according to his abilities, or his programming, as Carlo would have it. Xweft was the chief linguist and ambassador who took charge of them and graciously provided all they required. Early in their stay he took them to meet the Co-ordinator, who appeared to be the chief, and who seemed honoured by their visit. He and other Xenobians understood a little of what they said, but Xweft was growing fluent.

A few days after their arrival they were sitting in their room in the Xenobian equivalent of a hotel, while Jan carefully analysed the vegetation supplied for their food, setting aside the few items which would prove poisonous to humans.

'I'm still confused about what goes on in the city,' Peter admitted, recalling all they had been shown there that day.

'It's so clean and well-organised,' Carlo approved.

Peter was not satisfied. He needed to find some underlying purpose to justify all the sweepings and tidyings performed by its industrious inhabitants.

Carlo voiced his suspicions that the creatures might be mechanical. Besides the occasional jerkiness in their movement he had noticed that they did not seem to consume the vegetation, like animals, but ingest some kind of oily fuel they had elaborately processed.

Jan shared his curiosity. 'They draw their knowledge from the vast databases on their computers,' he mused, munching some tender fresh roots of local vegetation. 'I doubt if they think independently. And I've seen no evidence of music or drama.'

'Do they have any leisure?' Peter asked. 'Xweft seems to be on call all day.'

'What about that Art Gallery he showed us?' Carlo said suddenly. 'The pictures were rather formal, but someone must have painted them.'

'That building was ancient,' Jan reminded them, 'older than anywhere else in the city. And have you ever seen one of these creatures actually drawing or painting?' The others shook their heads.

'I don't believe these are the same beings who sent the Message,' Peter asserted.

'They look the same,' Jan said. 'They're just like the bipeds in that diagram that came through space.'

Their speculation was resolved the following day, when the three of them observed the recharging process and were taken to the Warehouse: the creatures were unquestionably androids.

The morning after that revelation Xweft met them in the hotel lobby. 'Little to see today,' he said. 'Xenobians not work much. Today we rest and think of the Elders.'

'Who are the Elders?' demanded Carlo.

'They are the Great Ones who made us in their own image,' Xweft told them.

'Did they send the Message?' Asked Peter urgently.

'What Message?' Asked Xweft. It had surprised them that with all his friendliness, his breadth of knowledge and his willingness to let them browse through the great databases of stored information, he seemed unaware of the Message beamed in Earth's direction.

'Can we meet the Elders?' Jan asked him.

'Not possible. Elders gone away since many years.' Xweft seemed uneasy. 'Some went in spaceships.'

'They might have stuck around to meet us once they'd sent the Message,' grumbled Carlo.

'Never question wisdom of the Elders,' Xweft said with uncharacteristic annoyance. 'Must trust.'

Peter felt they were on the verge of a vital discovery. 'When did you last see your Elders?' he pressed Xweft.

'Many years since,' Xweft repeated. 'During Technology Margin.'

'What's the Technology Margin?' asked Carlo.

'We hold information about other planets observed by Elders,' Xweft told them. 'Beings on advanced planets develop nuclear power. Technology Margin lies between major life-forms splitting atom and destroying themselves with nuclear weapons.'

Jan's eyes widened. 'Other planets have nuclear power?' He asked. 'You measure their – er – Technology Margin and keep the figures on your computers?'

'Some planets survive many decades in Technology Margin,' Xweft assured them.

'What's the maximum number of years any planet has lasted?' Peter could not help asking.

'So far maximum two hundred and twenty years,' Xweft told them promptly.

For a few moments they digested this information. 'I want to understand the history of your planet,' Peter told Xweft. 'I'd like to see your records of the nuclear war here, and your most recent information about the Elders.'

'I help you find data,' Xweft agreed. 'Little in those sections. Nuclear war most bad time. Not many records kept.'

Xweft took them into a large air-conditioned room where stored knowledge could be accessed from the computer. He typed in requests for them in Xenobian and translated the information as it appeared on the screen. Peter's spirits sank as sketchy records were accessed of the events leading to the nuclear war. It was becoming all too clear who had created the androids, who had sent the Message, and what had happened to them.

'I'd have liked to meet your Elders,' he told Xweft.

'We too. But one day they come again. We watch constantly. When your ship arrived we thought Elders coming, but you not quite like Them.'

Jan fidgeted. 'Haven't we seen enough about the nuclear war?' He said. 'I want to know more about other planets. You say that your Elders travelled to them?'

'A few Elders set off in ships.'

'Can we see a Xenobian spaceship?' Carlo asked. 'I want to compare the technology.'

'None in use,' Xweft said. 'All in use just before war.'

'Show us the specification,' Jan suggested.

'Sorry – not entered on database,' Xweft said. 'Much left out at time of great trouble.' He browsed through the records of their contacts with other planets. There were no details of the technology used to send messages, but the information received concerning other life-forms was fascinating, and Jan made copious notes until they grew tired and returned to the hotel.

'We've got a breakthrough after all!' Jan gloated as they settled in their room. 'One other planet with intelligent life is within travelling distance of Earth. With the Xenobian's data banks and our capacity to travel across space, we're on the verge of fresh discoveries.'

'If we don't arrive too late again,' Peter said gloomily.

Their door opened and an android stepped in. 'Message arrived from your planet,' he announced. Two other androids carried in a bullet-shaped communication pod.

'Thank you,' Carlo dismissed them. Peter and Jan watched curiously as he opened it. To reach them so quickly the message must have been sent soon after they had set out from Earth.

Carlo's face clouded. 'We're recalled,' he announced. '"Return at once. International situation grave."' He read.

Jan swore. 'Just as we're getting valuable facts about other planets,' he complained. 'I vote we stay another week and collect more data from the computer.'

'You heard Luke's orders,' Carlo overruled him. 'We start preparing the ship tonight and tomorrow we set off. Besides, we knew we shouldn't stay long with this level of radiation.'

'Suppose there's nuclear war by the time we return. Shouldn't we stay here?'

Peter made himself face this eventuality. 'Wouldn't you want to get back to be with your family? I would.'

The next day the Co-ordinator and other high-ranking androids came to the launch pad to bid them farewell, but Peter was disappointed that Xweft was missing. He had tried to persuade the others to take the sociable android with them to Earth, but Jan had complained that there was not enough space in the ship for his long limbs and Carlo had suggested Xweft would pose a security risk.

'Come off it!' Peter had protested. 'What do you expect him to do, pull out a laser gun and hijack the ship?'

'Precisely. He might want to set out in search of his Elders.'

Peter sighed. 'He could be right about the Second Coming,' he said. 'The Elders who were in space when the war began may have survived, and they or their descendants may yet return.'

Just as they were about to close the hatch the tall figure of Xweft came rushing towards them. 'Excuse I am late,' he said. 'I gave you inaccurate data. Urgent to get it corrected.'

Peter would miss that gruff voice. 'What is it, Xweft?'

'That figure I gave you for Technology Margin – it was not corrected for year length on Earth.'

'So what's the adjusted figure?'

'In Earth years maximum Technology margin so far is one hundred and nineteen years.'

Peter clasped his hand and muttered a hurried farewell. They closed the hatch and Jan began the ignition sequence with some haste. Time was running short.

Stars in the Water

by Andrea Tang

'Here we are.'

In a South American marine research facility, Dr Warren Harding and Dr Len Dresmon stopped at one of the glass windows of a large aquarium tank. Looking through the glass pane of the tank, the two marine biologists spotted a strange formless figure in the blue water. It floated motionlessly.

'This is Tetra,' Harding announced.

'Magnificent...' Dresmon remarked, taking a step closer to the glass to get a better look at the oddity.

'She's not moving much right now, but there are times when she's quite active,' Harding informed.

Dresmon looked at him curiously. 'She? You've gendered it?'

Harding looked away and rubbed his arm sheepishly. 'Well, not exactly. It's just that she seems female to me for some reason.'

Dresmon chuckled. 'Don't fall in love with the specimen, Warren.'

Harding laughed lightly. 'I don't think that would be possible.'

Dresmon's attention returned to the formless creature in the tank. It was of an undefined shape, a large man-sized blob of misty transparency. Its surface appeared like delicate membrane. It made Dresmon think of a jellyfish without tentacles. At its centre was the only discernable organ. Some kind of heart, Dresmon thought. And around that heart there were internal sources of light: luminous bright blue spots that were concentrated at the creature's core but seemed to spread out in lines across its whole form.

'This is definitely an amazing discovery,' Dresmon commented. 'In all my years of studying marine invertebrates, I don't think I've ever seen anything quite like this. It's kind of jellyfish-like, but it doesn't appear to have a fixed, solid form.'

'Yes, the intriguing thing is that Tetra has shape-shifting abilities,' Harding replied. 'She can alter her size and form to a complex degree. She's capable of disguise. We've observed her adopting the forms of several kinds of marine life before: sea anemones, starfish, octopus, fish, even dolphins. Her shape-shifting ability could be a survival or hunting mechanism, or perhaps...even a form of communication.'

'Remarkable. And the fluorescent patterns, they're quite striking too.'

'That's what we named her on: "Tetra" from the tropical aquarium fish "neon tetra", characterized by a bright blue stripe running across its body.'

'Fitting.'

Dresmon peered closer at the creature's centre. As he did, Tetra drifted backwards in the water slightly. Harding noted this.

'It only seems to have one central organ,' Dresmon observed aloud. 'Kind of like a giant amoeba in some ways.'

'From what I've seen, Tetra's a lot more advanced than a single-celled organism,' Harding mildly protested.

'How so?' Dresmon's gaze remained on Tetra as he asked. The edges of her shapeless translucent form quivered.

'She displays signs of intelligence,' Harding explained. 'She's naturally inquisitive, often responds to our presence. I think she likes to watch us back, sometimes.'

Dresmon's gaze narrowed, scrutinizing Tetra. 'You suggest it has sight, but I don't see any signs of developed eyes. It's possible that it possesses some form of ocelli eyespot cells that allow it to respond to light though, like many jellyfish.'

'I'm certain she perceives us somehow. She may have a wide field of vision or at least some kind of sophisticated sensory system. It's my belief that she can see or sense us with every part of her body.'

Dresmon touched his chin in thought. 'Interesting theory.' He paused. 'So this creature was found off the coast of the Falkland Islands you say?'

'Yes, caught by trawlers from the east side. They were quite surprised when they hauled her up to their boat. They'd never seen anything like her.'

'And this was the only one they saw at the time?'

Harding nodded. 'Yes, she was the only one in the net. At first they thought they'd caught a large shark. She had taken the shape of a large fish. But upon closer inspection, they realised her entire body was transparent, unlike any known shark. We were contacted soon after about their discovery.'

Suddenly Tetra became agitated. She condensed herself into a compact ball then expanded into a large inkblot shape. Dresmon watched this with fascination. Harding sensed that she was uneasy.

'Well I think we can safely say that this is an entirely new species of marine creature,' Dresmon declared, 'unlike anything known. Intelligent, free-formed and luminous. There's a good chance it'll warrant its own unique classification. We'll need to collect more data on it for sure. I think this could really be the find of the century, Warren.'

Harding looked at Tetra quietly for a moment, becoming lost in thought. 'A new form of marine life...' He trailed off, watching Tetra settle again into a relaxed undefined form.

'Warren?' Dresmon prompted when his companion fell silent.

Harding turned back to him. 'I know this might sound a little crazy, but sometimes... I think she's trying to tell us something, like trying to communicate a message, but we don't understand her. I've thought that maybe... she's not quite what we think she is. I get this feeling that she's more like a sentient being than a creature. She seems to study us as much as we study her. What if... What if she's from another civilisation? Like another advanced race? What if she's not originally native to Earth?'

'Would these ideas be coming from the same sense that tells you this organism is female?' Dresmon inquired humorously. 'Don't you think it's a little early to be getting carried away with fanciful notions? Perhaps it'd be best if we just focus on finding out more about the physiology and behaviour of this creature for the time being before we jump to sci-fi-type conclusions of it being some kind of alien life-form, hmm?'

'Yeah, I guess.' Harding's tone was uncertain.

'Look, you've obviously been spending a lot of time with "Tetra" here and I'm sure you've observed plenty of fascinating and inexplicable behaviour from "her", but let's try and stay down to earth and grounded in reality. There's just no evidence yet for what you're proposing, that she could be from some other race or world. I think you may be over-analyzing unfamiliar, but simple behaviours. It's always interesting to look for signs of intelligence and human-like traits in other living creatures, but it's unlikely that any of them are on the same level as us. Don't let yourself get carried away with your imagination, Warren. We're scientists remember? And we stick to facts and hard data on what we study.'

'Haven't you ever wondered though,' Harding questioned distantly, 'how we would recognise an alien on our planet if there ever were any? If they couldn't communicate directly with us and were lost on our world, amongst our wildlife, adapting to survive like life on Earth, how could we tell them apart from out native creatures? How would we tell if a form of life truly came from Earth or elsewhere? Could we really recognise advanced life-forms? Or would we automatically assume anything which we cannot directly relate to be lesser creatures?'

'Aliens coming to Earth and hiding amongst our wildlife?' Dresmon chuckled. 'Sounds like a great story idea.' He then raised his wrist and glanced down at a watch. 'Oh! I gotta get going. I have another appointment.'

'Sure, Len. I'll see you again soon.'

Dresmon made his way to the exit of the tank room. 'Keep me updated on Tetra,' he shouted back.

'Sure thing. You'll hear from me soon,' Harding returned with a wave.

'Don't stay in the water with her too long,' Dresmon joked as he opened the door. 'See you later.' He walked out.

Now alone, Harding turned back to Tetra. Approaching the tank glass, he gazed at her undefined form. She floated toward him and her form began to change again. She stretched vertically, making herself taller. Then to Harding's surprise, her lower half split into two leg-like appendages. Then from her sides a pair of arms separated. A head took shape from the top of her new form. Harding gasped. Before him, Tetra had taken on a humanoid form for the first time. He stepped back. Tetra lifted an arm. As she did, fingered hands formed from the ends of her arms. She touched the glass of her tank with thin translucent fingers. Harding was stunned. For a moment, he stood paralysed, staring. Tetra's fingers did not move from the glass. She remained like a frozen statue, still in the water, seemingly waiting. Curiosity and wonder urged Harding forward. He moved slowly toward her. When he was right up to the glass, he raised a hand tentatively and brought it up to Tetra's. He laid his palm upon the outline of hers and simultaneously, on either side of the glass, their hands pressed together. Their bodies mirrored each other perfectly.

'What are you?' Harding whispered.

Tetra's hand pulled away from the glass and she began to rise to the surface of the water. On instinct, Harding rushed to a metal ladder against the side of the tank. He pulled himself to the top and looked down into the gently ebbing waters. Tetra surfaced, her cloudy translucent skin glistening. She drew near to Harding and raised a hand out of the water to him. Slowly, Harding reached for her. Their fingertips made contact. Then Tetra's hand wrapped around Harding's and before he could react, it dissolved and engulfed his arm. Her aqueous form travelled up to his shoulder then washed up his neck toward his face. Strangely, Harding felt no fear. To his mild surprise, she felt warm and smooth, like running oil as she streamed frictionlessly up his skin. She glided over his cheek. An unexplainable connection was made. Harding sensed sensations and feelings – Tetra's. His eyes closed and for a timeless moment he was aware only of her otherworldly touch.

Help me.

Harding could hear it like a resonant echo, her calling. His eyes snapped opened again and he found himself face to face with Tetra. Her fluid and featureless face offered no expressions to read or windows into the soul, yet Harding knew what it was she was feeling. Uncertainty, desperation, fear and isolation had been long present in her, but now a glimmer of hope also was manifesting that came from making contact with him. Harding's gaze was drawn down into the depths of her flowing, veil-like being. His mouth opened in awe. A milky way of bioluminescent stars glowed vibrantly from within her. Before his eyes, a galaxy grew in size, pulsing in rhythm with an alien heartbeat. It was alive and full of possibilities.

How Do You Feel?

by Robert Leonard

'Vasily...wake up, Vasily.'

Vasily Pavlov opened his eyes to find his bedroom dancing about as his mother shook him awake.

'Mum: it's Saturday – there's no school on Saturday.'

He lay back down, but his mother was insistent. 'Vasily – get up; you have a visitor – an official visitor. It's something to do with that competition you entered.'

'Have I won something?' he asked.

'I think so...perhaps...I'm not sure. Put your dressing-gown on and come downstairs.'

Vasily leapt out of bed and shrugged his way into the thick dressing-gown that his mother kept promising him he would grow into, and followed her downstairs.

When he reached the hallway, Vasily jumped from rug to rug, so that he wouldn't have to walk barefoot on the cold stones, and nervously entered the front room.

Murmured chatter stopped as soon as he arrived and all eyes turned towards him. His mother and father were perched on the edge of the sofa like a pair of parakeets.

Sitting comfortably in the armchair opposite his parents was a very old woman. She had a twinkle in her eye and she was smiling at him.

'Good morning, Vasily,' she said. 'I'm sorry to get you out of bed so early on a Saturday morning. My name is Sofia Tereshkova. I am Director of Exopsychology at the Moscow Institute of Advanced Learning and I wanted to congratulate you personally on winning the Chocolate Star breakfast cereal competition.'

'What competition is that, Vasily?' his father asked.

'I will explain,' Sofia said before Vasily could reply. 'As everyone knows, who has not been living in a nuclear bunker for the past forty years, the Earth is engaged in extensive communication with alien beings from the Gliese-581 star system. These communications have all been coordinated by the United Nations and, up until now, they have only involved senior members of the scientific community – mathematicians, physicists and the like.'

'And psychologists?' Vasily asked shrewdly.

Sofia smiled and nodded. 'Yes; and psychologists – also biologists and chemists, and they have been asking very deep and profound questions of our new-found friends. But they all have one thing in common – they are all quite old: not many as old as me perhaps, but quite old nevertheless. This being the case, I thought it might be fun to ask a younger person to pose a question for them. How old are you, Vasily?'

'I'm ten – nearly eleven.'

'Ten - nearly eleven: very good. So I persuaded the Chocolate Star breakfast company to run a little competition for me and I thought your question was the best, Vasily.'

'What was the question?' his father asked.

'How do you feel?' Vasily replied.

'I feel fine, thank you very much,' his father retorted, gruffly, 'but what was the question?'

'That was the question, Dad. "How do you feel?"' Vasily explained.

His father frowned. 'Not much of a question, that: was there only one entry to this competition then?'

'Actually, there were a great many entries,' Sofia assured him, 'and Vasily's was the best. Let me explain. To begin with; it is what we call an open question. What is one plus one? That is a closed question – there is only one answer and that answer is either right or wrong – end of story. But with an open question, the answer can go on as long as you like and Vasily's question works on several different levels. Can you think what some of them are, Vasily?'

'Well, it could mean: "do you have nerves and stuff in your fingers, for feeling with?" Or it could mean: "do you feel well? Do you have a head-ache, or stomach-ache?" Or it could mean: "do you feel happy, or sad?"'

Sophia nodded in agreement. 'So you see, there are many possible answers to this simple little question, and how they answer could tell us a lot about them.'

'So, you're going to send his question into space then?' his mother asked.

'Yes indeed,' Sophia answered.

'Well that's wonderful. When do you think he'll get a reply?'

Sophia chuckled at this and said, 'Vasily; why don't you tell your mother about the Gliese-581 star system?'

'OK. Gliese-581 is a red dwarf star, so it's smaller and cooler than our sun. It's about twenty light-years from Earth. That means my question will take twenty years to get there and their answer will take twenty years to get back.'

'Gracious,' said his mother, 'that is a long time.'

'Well, Gliese-581 has lots of planets orbiting it, but there's only one that sits in the Goldilocks zone – that's the place where it's not too hot and not too cold, so people and things can live there – and that's called Gliese-581g. I call it Gee-gee for short. It's about three times bigger than the Earth and it orbits really close to its sun – a whole year only takes about thirty-seven days, and it doesn't spin like we do – one side faces the sun all the time and the other side is always dark – just like our moon.'

As Vasily prattled on, Sophia smiled inwardly. His enthusiasm – his passion for his subject – was infectious. It was more than she could have hoped for.

When Vasily eventually fell silent, Sophia nearly burst out laughing at the expression on his parents' faces. Instead she said, 'Vasily – you and your parents are invited to attend the transmission ceremony, where you will press the button that will send your message out into space. You will receive a certificate to mark the occasion. Also, with your parents' permission, I would like to offer you a full scholarship to the Moscow Academy of Learning. Who knows; if you work hard, you may become head of the Exopsychology department yourself some day.'

'Doctor Pavlov! Doctor Pavlov – wait!'

Vasily turned and saw Natalia Baronova, the head of Astrophysics, sprinting down the corridor towards him.

'What's up, Natalia?' he asked.

'The United Nations Communications Directorate has just sent through another batch of data from Gliese-581g: and Vasily, you won't believe it, they've answered your question – it has arrived at last.'

'You're right, Natalia: I don't believe it. Who put you up to it? Was it Pavel? Or Vladimir? – He always likes a good joke.'

Natalia opened her mouth to speak, but no sound came out. Instead, she grabbed his hand and hauled him back down the corridor, like a mother with a reluctant toddler in a supermarket.

When they reached the Communications room he could see at once that Natalia had been telling the truth. The giant multi-screens were teeming with downloading data.

Vasily keyed in a simple set of search parameters and then: there it was – his question. "Vasily Pavlov from Moscow asks: how do you feel?"

In a daze, he read the answer. "The beings on Gliese-581g feel by means of a series of neuroreceptors located in dorsal, ventral and lateral arrays. We are in good health and are feeling fine."

Vasily turned to Natalia and said, 'This answer has arrived four years too soon.'

Natalia looked at him with a puzzled expression. 'What do you mean Vasily...four years too soon? Do you mean this is not in answer to your question?'

'Oh, it's in answer to my question alright,' Vasily assured her. 'However, my question was sent when I was ten years old. Gliese-581g is twenty light-years from Earth; so it takes twenty years for the message to reach them and then another twenty years for the reply to get back – making forty years in total. So I was not expecting an answer until I am at least fifty and I'm only forty-six – hence, it's four years early.'

'But that's not possible, Vasily,' Natalia said. 'For a message to get to Gliese-581g and back in less than forty years would necessitate it travelling faster than light for at least part of its journey and that's just not physically possible.'

'I agree, Natalia,' Vasily said. 'So we must look for an alternative explanation that is possible.'

Natalia frowned in concentration. 'Alright – if we accept that the round-trip took thirty-six years instead of forty, then the source of this data can't be more than eighteen light-years away. If I compare the frequency of this transmission with the frequency of older transmissions, I should be able to tell if the source is moving.'

Natalia initiated several screens and started manipulating data. She worked quickly for several minutes and when she had finished, Vasily thought she looked pale.

'The frequency of this latest transmission has a significant blue-shift compared to earlier transmissions. If my calculations are correct, then the source is moving towards us at approximately half the speed of light.'

'Can you tell where it would be now?' Vasily asked.

'If it has maintained a constant speed, then in the eighteen years that it has taken your message to reach Earth, the source will have advanced another nine light-years, which would put it about nine light-years from Earth. If it keeps going at the same rate, then it will get here in eighteen years from now.'

Vasily found that he couldn't think straight. He felt the enormity of what they had found weighing him down, so he returned to the answer to his question.

'They start by saying: "the beings from Gliese-581g", as though they're talking about somebody else. But then they go on to say: "...we are feeling fine", which would indicate that they are now talking about themselves. That doesn't make a lot of sense.'

Natalia was saved the trouble of thinking of a reply by the arrival of Anna Ulanova, from the Department of Exobiology, and Sergey Middendorf, from the Mathematics Department.

'Congratulations, Vasily,' said Anna.

'Have you cracked the code yet?' asked Sergey.

'Thanks, Anna. What code?' Vasily replied.

'There's a big chunk at the end of the data-stream that's encrypted – you need a sixteen character code to unlock it, so I thought I'd ask our resident Psychologist why our good friends from Gliese-581g would suddenly send us information in a code that's nigh-on uncrackable?'

'Uncrackable?' queried Vasily.

'We could hit it with our most powerful computers for a thousand years and not even dent it,' Sergey told him.

'Then it must be something you don't need a computer for,' Vasily said.

'My thoughts exactly,' said Sergey, bringing up the code entry parameters on another screen.

Vasily shrugged and typed in: "How do you feel?"

For a moment, nothing happened. Then a message came up saying: "Invalid entry".

'Try it in Cyrillic,' joked Anna.

Vasily did as she suggested and the screen filled with data.

'Look!' exclaimed Anna, 'there are photographs of people! Look at those muscles – gravity there must be significantly greater than on earth.'

'What are the chances that the people on Gliese-581g would look just like us?' asked Vasily.

'Pretty slim,' Anna told him. 'Early on, we sent them a complete human genome. Perhaps they've managed to "clone" some humans from the data we sent. They look like a boy and a girl – about eighteen years old, I'd say.'

'That would explain their answer to my question,' Vasily said. 'They referred to the inhabitants of Gliese-581g in the third person, but also said: "we are feeling fine". That's very clever. If you're right, Anna, the people of Gliese-581g are sending human beings, who have lived amongst them for eighteen years, to make first contact with us. They must realise we'll be more comfortable interacting with people like us, rather than a bunch of aliens.'

'What do you mean – "sending"?' Sergey asked.

'We think they're on their way here now,' Natalia said, without taking her eyes off the screen she was working on. 'I'm trying to use the old James Webb telescope to find their ship. It mostly sees in the infra-red part of the spectrum, so I've told it to look between Earth and Gliese-581 and lock onto the hottest thing it can find.'

'Can it see anything that far out?' Anna asked.

'Are you kidding? The poor thing's going cross-eyed trying to look for something that close.'

A few minutes later the red glow of a false-colour image appeared on the screen and Natalia shouted, 'Got it! Boy, that thing's hot. It's as though they want us to find them.'

'Perhaps they do,' Vasily said.

'How fast are they travelling?' Sergey asked.

'Half light-speed,' Natalia replied.

'So it will take forty years for them to get here from Gliese-581g,' said Anna. 'If they were eighteen when they set off, they'll be fifty-eight when they arrive.'

'No, no, no.' Sergey shook his head vigorously. 'It will take us forty years for them to travel that distance. But at half light-speed, relativity will have a profound effect on them. Trust me – they'll be much less than fifty-eight when they arrive.'

'Vasily, what else would make people more comfortable with all this?' Anna asked.

'Well, if first physical contact was made out in space – in orbit around Mars, perhaps, that might help. That way, people could check out their space-ship and make sure it isn't armed with weapons of global destruction.'

'We could set up a quarantine zone,' Anna said. 'We could inoculate them against normal human diseases and screen them for anything they may have brought with them.'

'Good idea,' Vasily said. 'Now, we need to formulate a reply to send back out into space.'

'But won't that give the game away?' asked Anna.

'We could encrypt the message the same way they did,' Sergey suggested. 'If anyone asks, we can just tell them we want to see if they can crack our code.'

'How are we going to break the news to people?' Natalia asked. 'We're going to have to tell them eventually.'

'I think we should let Pavel Lenz do that for us,' Vasily said.

'What, Pavel Lenz the movie producer?' queried Anna.

'Yes,' Vasily confirmed. 'We invite him here and we tell him everything. If he makes a movie about our discovery and gets people used to the idea of a peaceful interaction between ourselves and the ambassadors from Gliese-581g, then it will be easier for them to accept the reality of the situation when we are ready to reveal it to them.'

'If there's going to be a movie, I want one percent of the gross,' said Sergey.

'Be serious, Sergey,' Natalia admonished.

'I am being serious.'

'If there's anything to share, we'll all share it equally,' Vasily said. 'In the meantime, we have to work hard and in complete secrecy.'

'Once we've sent the next message, how long before we can expect a reply?' Anna asked.

'Our next message will reach their space-craft when they are about six light-years from Earth.' Natalia said. 'If they answer promptly, then we'll receive an answer about six years after that – so twelve years from now.'

'Well, at least we know they're feeling fine,' said Anna.

'Not necessarily,' Vasily replied. 'We know they felt fine eighteen years ago. I think I'm going to ask them again: "how do you feel?"'

Protocol 909

by Peter Rolls

Bzzz, bzzz…

The red phone buzzed and the General snatched up the handpiece. 'Bishop.'

The caller's voice was crisp. 'It's Jensen, sir – at Wolf Lake. I think you should come over. I'm invoking Protocol 909 …'

The General pumped his fist in silent triumph. '909? Are you serious? This isn't some fancy kite-flying?'

'Needs your attention, sir.'

'With you in an hour.'

The General looked hard and looked again 'You've checked all this out? … It's not a local glitch – or some radio-ham jokester?'

'No chance,' said Jensen. 'I fed the co-ordinates to our auto-link set-ups at El Diablo and Zebedee. They give the same profile.' He spread out two more record-strips.

The General made up his mind. 'OK. This is the biggie. And it's on my watch …' He did a double fist-pump. 'The rulebook says we put this straight up the line. Pack your bag.'

Bzzz, bzzz…

The Secretary of State woke from a tropical-beach dream, breathed hard and picked up her phone. 'Mackay.'

'General Bishop here, Madam Secretary. I'm invoking Protocol 909.'

'909? Are you serious?'

'Serious … you betcha!' The General was in an all-action, gum-chewing mood. 'I have a flight waiting and will be with you by three am your time.'

'OK, I'll be in my office.'

Bzzz, bzzz…

The President turned on his pillow and jabbed the speaker-phone. 'Foster.'

'Secretary Mackay here, Mr President. I'm sorry to wake you, but I have General Bishop with me – and a colleague from Wolf Lake.'

'At this time of night?'

'He's invoking Protocol 909, sir.'

'909! Are you serious? I thought we'd pulled the plug.'

'This seems to be a residual. Mr President.'

'Residual! Some goddam bureaucratic leftover.'

'I believe it needs your urgent attention, sir.'

'OK, Oval Office in ten.'

Jensen put the player on the President's desk. 'We're on a mapping survey, sir – with our Deep Space Radio Array. Two days ago, we picked up this signal. It's running day and night, but I'll give you a few seconds.' He started the playback …

> *bezeepzbzeezpzbezezpzzzzzbezeepzbzeezpzzzzzbezeepzzzz…*
> *bezeepzbzeezpzbezezpzzzzzbezeepzbzeezpzzzzzbezeepzzzz…*

'Is that it?' The President looked sharply at Jensen.

'That's the original, sir – including background noise. But I have a cleaned up version …'

> *beeeep, beeeep, beeeep…zzzzz… beeeep, beeeep…zzzzz… beeeep…zzzzz… beeeep, beeeep, beeeep…zzzzz… beeeep, beeeep…zzzzz… beeeep…zzzzz…*

'It goes on like that, sir – three beeps, two beeps, one beep.' He unrolled the paper trace records. 'Three-two-one … day and night.'

The President wasn't impressed. 'Surely it's some – whaddya call it – cosmicality. A pulsar, quasar, whatever …'

'Not in this wave-band, sir. Not with this transmit pattern.'

'Where's it coming from …?'

'Not sure, sir. Could be Gliese 581.'

'Gliese 581?'

'A red dwarf star, sir. It has several planets and the thinking is that one of them might be habitable. It's around 20 light-years away.'

'Give it to me in miles, for crissake. I need to get a handle on this thing.'

'Around 120 trillion miles, sir.' Jensen wrote down the figures and passed the paper to the President.

'That's a lot of noughts.'

'Sure is, sir. Thirteen of them.'

The President shook his head in almost-disbelief. 'So you're saying this stuff has been coming on to us at the speed of light for 20 years?'

'Maybe long before that.'

'Why us?'

'Good question, sir. They – whoever or whatever they are – may have picked up some sign of activity. Radio or TV signals – could be … Atomic explosions, more likely.'

The President clutched the air with both hands. 'Just a goddam cherry-picking minute, mister. When you say 'whoever or whatever', please don't tell me you're talking little green men.'

Jensen looked unhappy. 'It's not my area, sir. But I'd say they're not necessarily green. Or little. And maybe not 'men' as we know them. One thing's for sure – they're way, way ahead of us technically.'

'Let me get this straight. If we could somehow send an answer to these Gliese guys, it would arrive in around 20 years. And, if they got straight on the case, we'd hear back in 40 years time.'

Jensen inspected his nails. 'That's the theory, sir.'

The President looked at the Secretary. 'So we'd get forty years minimum … Around ten presidential terms, right?'

She met his gaze. 'So what do we do?'

The President's eye flicked at Jensen and the General. 'Who knows about this?'

'Just the four of us,' said Jensen.

'OK,' said the President. 'Here and now, we tell no-one – right? We set up a Study Group. Tight focus.'

'Time-frame?' said the Secretary.

The President checked his diary. I'm pressing-the-flesh in Chicago tomorrow. Friday, I'm up-state, shooting things. Make it Monday …'

The Secretary's eyebrows lifted. 'Short notice, sir. We need a top team on this.'

The President clicked his fingers. 'I'm not talking Inaugural Address here, or some goddam Congressional paper-mountain. I need a single-sheet summary … Problem, Solutions. Upside, Downside ... OK?'

'I'm on it, sir.'

Saturday morning

The Secretary of State tapped the table. 'OK, team. I'm sorry for the short notice. Let's get to it.'

They squared their note-pads and began doodling.

This Group is asked to make recommendations reference the signal received at Wolf Lake. You've read the outline: you've signed the no-tell.' She drew a finger across her throat. 'Our Codeword is Mandrake 909. Security level is Phoenix Ultra, which is as high as it goes – and then some. OK?'

They got the message.

'The President expects our recommendations on Monday. Which gives us two days. Right?'

They sighed and poured themselves ice-water.

'First off, let's have a round-the -table Who's Who …' Her steel-rimmed glasses levelled at them in turn. 'I am Marilyn Mackay, Secretary of State.'

The bulky, gum-chewing soldier was 'General Bishop, Army Air Corps.'

The gangly young nail-biter was 'Joe Jensen, Radio Astronomy Facility, Wolf Lake.'

The woman with big hair and chunky jewellery was 'Gudrun Torjussen, Professor in Astrodynamics at MIT.'

The crew-cut pencil-twiddler was 'Carlos Sanchez, Office of Culture and Communication.'

The Secretary ticked boxes. 'OK, team. Let's get to it ... Indications are that we have an alien radio source operating at a distance of 20 light-years. Which, in old money, is 120 trillion miles.'

They doodled noughts.

She checked agenda items, 'Draft structure for discussion: *Item One* … Is this Friend or Foe? *Item Two* … Should we reply? If so, how? What do we say and how do we say it? *Item Three* … Upside. Potential benefits. *Item Four* … Downside. Threats and counter-measures. *Item Five* … Budgets and timescales. Finally … And this is a biggie – do we make this thing public?'

The Professor said, 'For this, we have two days? I give you answer in two seconds … Forget it. Whatever we need to do, we don't know how and we can't afford it.' She doodled dark clouds and said no more.

The Secretary of State worked her steel-rimmed look round the room. 'Any more thoughts? Does anyone take this thing as a 'positive'?'

Sanchez the Culture man said 'Could be ...'

The General's fist banged the table 'Sure thing, buster. It could be curtains for the human race.'

'OK,' said the Secretary. 'Some variation of views here. That's constructive ...' She took refuge in a cloud of execu-buzz …. 'Let's keep focussed on outcomes. We need a fully-nuanced and closely-argued set of recommendations, going forward into the threat-opportunity nexus – OK? … Above all, we keep it short.' She drew breath and looked round the table. 'For starters, is this Friend or Foe?'

Sanchez the Culture man said 'Either way, maybe we should send a big smiley "Hello". Can we do that?'

Jensen puffed his cheeks. 'Not right now. We'd need to get into a few new areas – UHF generators and power-beam image-control and inter-stellar target acquisition and so on.' He spread his fingers wide. 'But, hey, it's an opportunity.'

The Secretary clicked her fingers. 'Cost? Time-frame? Ball-park at this stage.'

Jensen shrugged. 'Years – ten, maybe twenty. Dollars – a trillion, maybe two or three … I'll get back to you.'

‘Tomorrow, right?’ She looked round the table ‘OK, people – keeping on the ‘let's-do-it’ ticket, how do we speak with these guys. We have to get beyond the beep.’

‘Right,’ said Sanchez. ‘We may be looking at a non-verbal linguo-cultural exchange – and we have precedents here. Some tribes use click-noises; others have jungle drums.’

The Professor raised her eyebrows. ‘You're talking about a conversation with a there-and-back response time of forty-years.’

‘Sure thing,’ said Sanchez. ‘ExoLinguistics – it'll be a breakthrough. Maybe we start with click-beetles and work on up.’ He rubbed his hands. ‘This is Nobel Prize country.’

The General looked at the Professor. ‘OK. Let's forget the happy-fairy talk ... Worst case – if these are the bad guys, what might they have up their sleeves?’

She smiled a thin smile. ‘Three scenarios. One – they've got a ballistic gizmo, with nuclear-tipped or bio-plague warheads.’

The General shrugged. ‘What's new? We can match all that. So we go for first strike.’

She doodled star-symbols. ‘Problem is they're 120 trillion miles away. Whatever we launch at them will take a while to get there.’

‘How long?’

‘You do the math,’ she said. ‘Suppose – just suppose – we develop a space-vehicle to travel at, say, 100,000 miles an hour. How long will it take to travel 120 trillion miles?’

He pursed his lips. ‘You're the figures whizz. How long?’

She scribbled numbers. ‘Round figures – 130,000 years, but please check it out.’

The General wrote down the numbers and did the calculation in growing disbelief. ‘You mean we should have launched this thing 130,000 years ago?’

‘Earlier would have been better.’

‘So it was down to those goddam do-nothing Neanderthals.’ He snapped open a new pack of gum. ‘Stone Age bastards.’

The Professor got back to her thesis. ‘OK. Forget ballistic hardware – it's too slow and too clunky. We need to think Scenario Two – and this is the real killer ...’

The room fell quiet and she milked the moment. ‘Maybe they've got some sort of light-speed Death Ray. A gamma-hyperpulse, or anti-particle disintegrator – who knows. This could get here in 20 years.'

Faces froze.

The Professor was enjoying herself 'There's more.' She held up three fingers. 'Scenario 3 … What we've picked up may be a radio guidance beam.'

The General's mouth tightened. 'Like a laser target-marker?'

'Right. You see the marker, but never the bullet that hits you. Maybe the light-speed Planet Killer – whatever it is – is riding on a radio beam ... We can't see it and we can't stop it. Think of it as a lightning strike – times a billion.'

'*Coup de foudre*,' said Sanchez, the man from Culture and Communication.

'Ker-plunk,' said the General.

'And,' said the Professor 'as the Earth spins …'

'… we all fry together,' said Jensen.

They contemplated Earthdoom.

The Secretary sought to lift spirits. 'Sobering stuff, people … But is there an up-side here?'

Sanchez played a Culture card. 'Over a thousand years, we'd have maybe 25 'conversations'. We register this with UNESCO as a 'cultural exchange' and maybe get a grant-in-aid. Plus merchandising spin-off. We could squeeze big juice on this thing.'

The Secretary drew deep breath. 'Thanks for that, Mr Sanchez.' She looked round the table. 'That's it for now, folks. I figure we all need some major mull-time. Back here tomorrow at 9.00 sharp.'

Sunday morning

'OK, folks. Big day ahead. Let's have your thoughts – as a loosener. Keep them coming – as odd-ball and out-of-the-box as you like.'

The group let off their overnight steam …

The General raised a hand. 'I'm thinking way back to the Tunguska thing – maybe that was a sighting shot ... OK, it took out a chunk of Siberia – but we can live with that. These days, we could track a meteorite and nuke it before it hits us.'

… 'Let's not forget we have an election next year.'

… 'If we do anything, the whole world gets to know. The markets will fall off the cliff .'

… 'The Second Coming crazies will go into overdrive.'

… 'Yes, but how much actual damage. I mean – worst case – are we talking mega-seismics, firestorms, electroneuronics?'

… 'We have no way of knowing.'

… 'So we get worldwide casualties of what – a billion? Five-six billion? We can live with that. If we're ready for it.'

… 'What have we got in the works, weapon-wise?'

… 'I'm thinking deep bunkers – really deep.'

… 'DecisiMax just says Insufficient Data. It needs a few deaths.'

… 'Any of you guys see *Dr Strangelove*?'

… 'Keep to basics here. If it's some sort of electromagnetic whosit, we can't shoot it down and we can't dodge. We either deflect it – or we absorb it, So we're talking space-shields.'

… 'Which means we're talking cloud-cuckoo...'

… 'Anyone see *War of the Worlds*?'

… 'We're talking too many unknown unknown unknowns here.'

… 'Best strategy is to say nothing, do nothing. They might move on.'

… 'Dark matter – Higgs boson – do they come into the equation?'

The Secretary held up her hands. 'OK, team. That's enough brain-storms. We'll take a quick break and then get back to specifics.'

…

…

Monday morning

The Secretary laid a sheet of paper on the President's desk. 'You asked for a view on the 909 situation, sir.'

'Thank you, Marilyn.' The President picked up the sheet and gave it his full attention:

PHOENIX ULTRA

Mandrake 909

Upside – Optimax factors

- **Cultural benefits** Language and arts
- **Merchandising** Neo-product franchising

Downside – Pessimax factors

Potential Threat: Ballistic or Death Ray

- **Time frame** 130,000 or 0-20 years
- **Pandaemonium** Worldwide
- **Potential casualties**: Earthpop – estd. 7 billion
- **Collateral damage**: Earthmax – estd $1x10 15

Counteractive technology: ??

- Development costs $?tn
- Time scale ?yrs

Evaluation – Decisimax

- Insufficient firm data at this time

Recommendation:

- Do nothing. Say nothing.

PHOENIX ULTRA

The President nodded. 'Yes, that's pretty much my own thinking.' He looked at the Secretary. 'Please thank the Group for their expert attention and say that they can leave the matter with me.'

'Shall I alert the Vice-President, sir? Or the Joint Chiefs?'

He smiled a tight smile. 'With me, Madam Secretary.'

A week later

'Mr President, I'm sorry to disturb you. Wolf Lake have been on the line again. I think we may have an Imminence situation. They're getting single beeps now … It could be on a count-down, sir. Homing in …

*… zzz… **Beeeep** …zzz… **Beeeep** …zzz… **Beeeep** …zzz…*

The red light came on.

The room grew quiet.

The President took a sip of water.

The light switched to green.

The President flexed a smile for the camera. 'Fellow Americans … In recent days, there have been fanciful stories in the media of imminent global catastrophe.' His voice took on a cosy-fireside tone. 'I am speaking to you this evening to assure you that such rumours are comple …'

ZZZAPP … …

Searching for P'tach

by Andrew Irvine

I was the Leader of the Council of P'tach when we first heard from the Two-Legs. I can remember the fuss that the scientists made when they came to us and told us all about the signals from another star. Right from the start there was agitation in the Chamber, with tails rudely waving in the air and a distinct smell of fear, as voices were raised by some towards the back.

I was overjoyed to hear from them, even though we could not understand a word of their transmissions. The knowledge that there was definitely someone else out there; someone we could talk to, learn from and maybe teach things to, was just so exciting. I remember that there were some who warned of impending doom even then in the Great Chamber. Tulgen Isnech was among them right from the start, he was an old one even then, but I can remember his great voice echoing across the Chamber.

'Beware, fellow P'tachi, these voices, these people. Likely they will set out and come here in great monster space ships and destroy us. How many enemies do we already have? The slithering menarks come at us from all sides. The thunderous trolu shake the ground as they thunder over our heads. If we were not in our underground chambers we would not even survive. We should stop all radio transmissions and focus on defending our cities for the future when they come.'

He was a great orator, was Tulgen. I can picture him in the Chamber, raised up on his back legs with his middle legs waving in the air like another pair of arms, talking as if doom and destruction were already here.

I mocked him for his miserable outlook on life. Why assume the worst? If our life was so bad with our enemies around us, what did we have to lose? These people might be able to help us. We knew our technology was ahead of anything else on the planet, so we could talk to the aliens and get help against our enemies. The arguments raged on for a number of star-points and nothing was resolved, when we discovered that a group of Mulgi from the Western Hall of

Learning had been secretly beaming the aliens' transmissions back to them – a simple acknowledgement that they had been heard. After that, Old Tulgen and his daughter Bragik were to be heard almost daily berating the Mulgi for their "treacherous, foolhardy" act. They called for the punishment of the Mulgi – not just those in the Hall, but the whole community. Tulgen proclaimed that the Mulgi were trying to dictate policy for the whole planet. Whilst I could see that this was true, I thought that the damage, if any, was done and we needed the Mulgi on side to help us with the final part of the electro-wall to keep the menarks out of Mar-ah-ah for good. Their craftsmen were the best on the planet and we needed to be constructive. My will prevailed and Tulgen had to accept defeat on that. As you know, he is now one of the oldest of the Council – old and yellow he may be, but still to this day he holds a certain type of P'tach in thrall or so it seems.

Many @@@s later, when the Two-Legs arrived on our planet and we saw their immense size, there was no stopping the fear and the panic. People were smashing the radio equipment everywhere. They were shouting and jostling the Mulgi and it was hard to maintain any order. I am happy to say that there were no casualties and I managed to get a meeting together in the Great Chamber. However, as the reports came in of the great Two-legged creature zigzagging its way towards us across the Plain of Znya the populace would hear no reason at all. I told them that we needed to make ourselves known to them; that they were probably looking to greet us, like any intelligent being would. No, they wouldn't hear of it and I was voted out of the Chamber.

Councillor Bragik was made up to Leader and she set everyone to hiding our presence as much as possible. No-one was allowed to fly; nobody could make any kind of radio broadcasts and everywhere was searched for radio equipment. One poor soul had an ancient radio set in a storeroom and he was almost eaten by the mob, but I did, at least manage to protect him from harm. There was a total curfew, both here in Mar-ah-ah, and in the outlying cities and towns of our people. A few wise people in the Chamber managed to keep their place and do a little to prevent the worst bigotry. Darlach, an engineer from the successful electro-wall project, managed to keep a radio receiver going and get a team together to try and translate the radio signals we were picking up. From the direction and the equipment, it was clear the messages were being sent home and we recorded them all. Long afterwards we were able to analyse the messages in relation to what was going on at the time and feed it all into the computers. However, all we knew at the time was that the two-leg was walking along with strides arching over whole communities of P'tach, with a weight big enough to crush the roof in of any P'tachi chamber too close to the surface. I didn't realise it was possible for a living creature to be that big. The two-leg would work its way out from the spacecraft in ever-increasing circles and return to the craft after two-fifths of a day. The scientists hypothesised that this was the length of a day on their planet, as the Two-Legs consistently kept to this cycle, regardless of the light of day and night on our planet. We realised that this would have the advantage of observing the planet at all times of day and night. The scientists worked out that the next "day", the creature would be walking near us in Mar-ah-ah and indeed may walk right onto the city. At first the authorities tried to keep this quiet, but the word got out. Since flying was forbidden, no-one could travel far enough in the time available to escape the risk of being crushed, so everyone stayed put. People had felt secure in Mar-ah-ah, one of the few places where the Elagach could never break in, so people had dug closer to the surface. I managed to get an audience with Bragik, despite my expulsion and I persuaded her that there was no point in risking anybody's life near the surface, that if the creature's path was headed towards the City, everyone should be allowed, indeed encouraged to gather in the lowest chambers. Oh, the look in her eyes, the sneering tilt of her head.

'If it were not for the likes of you, we would not be in any danger. My whole city, thousands of people could be crushed in an instant.'

I remember her fat and hairy middle legs – for Bragik was an attractive P'tachi – out at her sides. Her inner eye shields were closed. You understand that in the upper circles of P'tachi hierarchy, this is very insulting, being a defensive gesture, suggesting that I might use violence on her. I tried to remain calm.

'Since you will not let us contact the creature, you cannot prove its intent is to harm us, so you have no proof of your accusation. Will you not rethink your actions in the moment of our greatest risk? One radio signal beamed at the spacecraft would show that we are intelligent beings. It is you Leader Bragik, who is putting us all at risk.'

'Signalling? Signalling? Guards, take him away, you heard him! If we are lucky they will not find us, but despite all our warnings you want to lead them right to us. Twenty P'tachi crushed in Mleth, yesterday. One hundred and twelve were injured and four died in groundquakes the day before. The entire community at M'gach wiped out in one vast footfall before that and this fool wants to put our capital at even greater risk. No, ex-Leader Antroi; I will take your advice about moving everyone down to the lowest chambers, but I will make certain that no messages are sent to the two-legged monsters,' She leaned forward until I could smell her hot breath, but had her arms across her neck – another very insulting defensive gesture. 'Very certain.'

I walked towards the guards with my arms upward to prevent the humiliation of the guards actually holding on to me. I was taken to the highest chamber where a number of my allies were already being held, so close to the surface that you could hear the sound of the wind through the ceiling. I am not sure what difference our proximity to the surface would have made if the city was trodden on, but it was a symbol of how little value was put on our lives. Over the next few hands of the sun, more people were cast into the chamber with us – my family, various people alleged to have supported the 'betrayal' of our city – scientists who originally broadcast messages out into the cosmos; people from the Western Hall; various scientists and others who were known to have been in favour of communicating with the aliens. They told us that the two-legs was on a direct path to the city and everyone other than us was being forcibly evacuated to the lowest chambers.

'Everyone?' said Darlach, who despite having been the darling of the city when the electro-wall had been switched on just a few star-points earlier, was now cast upwards with the rest of us. 'Are all the military going as well – all the guards that patrol the perimeter?'

'Everyone, as far as I can see,' replied my cousin Kchak, who was in the last batch of prisoners. 'They were to lock the doors on us, and go down to below the Great Stone, where everyone is now. They have remote cameras set up recording and observing and nobody will come up again until the two-legs has passed. The monster will be here in half a sun/hand.'

‘We will be crushed! Can’t we break open the door?’ Somebody yelled.

‘No, listen. We break open the ceiling and set a fire as a signal. There is nobody here to stop us,’ Darlach proposed.

Suddenly, we heard the sound like trolu, only in single steps, getting closer. *Thud. Thud! THUD! Thud! Thud* into the distance. In just a fraction of a sun/hand the creature had come past us and gone. It had missed the city by just the width of its tread, leaving a vast footprint half the size of a trolu just to one side of us.

Now the creature has gone, leaving us wondering – what could have happened? The hysteria passed and times have moved on. I stayed out of politics and I pass my time in the laboratory here, where we are working on the meaning of the radio messages we received. We are still not allowed to send any out.

...I searched the whole area of the planet on foot. I cannot find the city, the species or the source of the radio messages. It’s just vanished. Although there are various life forms, I can’t find anything bigger than a domestic cat and nothing with a glimmer of intelligence. I can only conclude that Singh was right, that the signals actually come from beyond this planet. It's strange that they appear to have come from exactly this area and that the signals stopped so abruptly when I arrived, but it’s departure time in 15 minutes, so that’s it for this planet for now.

The Decision

by Chris Sanderson

It was the end of the working day and the weekend lay ahead. Kessia murmured the repose command so the screen turned off and her seat turned towards the transwall, gradually reclining as it went. She took in a deep breath, briefly closed her eyes to clear her mind of work, and then leant back to look at the view in front of her. Because of Mercor's job, which required him to have quick access to the roofadrome, they were lucky enough to have an apartment on the two hundred and eightieth floor of the tower block. The whole outside wall was in transview material and she loved to gaze through it to watch the sky above the towers change its colours and gradually darken. Sometimes, despite the light pollution of the city, she could discern a bright star. At this time of year she might spot planet Jupiter whose moon, Europa, supported a scientific colony that had made contact with other worlds. Amazing to think that humans could be so far away and that beings from other worlds also travelled the universe when she rarely left even her home tower! She was happy though because everything she needed was here: towers were designed to provide all any individual needed, such as shops, restaurants, nurseries, health bases, exercise areas, entertainments and so on, all accessible by lifts and moving walkways. So she avoided going out into the packed walkways of the city or the underground system that led to further places.

Like most people she worked from her apartment through the screen but unlike most people, it was by choice. Highly qualified in her field of genome engineering, she had moved on from routine laboratory work to work that involved more contact with other people, by screen of course. After analysing the DNA graphs, she contacted the prospective parents to discuss the traits they wanted in their child and it was this face-to-face contact that she really enjoyed. Her work had given her a fascination for genetics with all its possibilities and she loved helping people with their choices. In her spare time she researched the history of repro-genetics and had become absorbed by stories of the past with its random, "natural" people. Until relatively recently you couldn't choose your child's looks and abilities: you simply took and learned to love whatever came your way. The dangers of this were obvious enough – vulnerability to disease, low intelligence, unsatisfactory physical appearance and so on – and yet there was something about it that appealed to her.

Before she met Mercor she had felt differently. Until then her relationships had been with men chosen the usual way – by the Matchmate programme: men she found interesting, but not as lasting partners. Her intention had been to wait until later to select one suitable to share a well-designed child with; but now here she was – only thirty, and in love with someone totally unlike herself, even, in some ways, quite odd. He was unusual looking, no doubt a "random" rather than a genetically selected individual – though she had never presumed to ask him. He had a large nose, bony forehead and very green eyes. They had met in the exercise area and it was his apparently never-waning energy that had attracted her attention. Rather short and wiry, he bounded enthusiastically from one exercise to another, always seeming happy. When their eyes met, she laughed and asked him why he was so lively. 'I'll tell you over a drink afterwards,' he had replied.

She later gathered that his physical fitness was due not only to his genes but also to his work. Always outside on the tower roofs and often physically demanding, it involved accessing and servicing the solar energy sources. He took the trickier assignments, where robots had failed. For quick and easy access, he had been given his own helivehicle and an apartment high in the tower. Using the terrestrial travel infrastructure would have been too time-consuming, given that some assignments were dealing with emergencies. Though much of his work was level two security, they had easily gained permission for her to move in with him, probably because her own job status was upper three level so she was already classified as trustworthy.

He was not on call this evening or over the weekend so she had decided today was a good time to tell him of her decision. Having rested for a few minutes, she took a shower, put on a flattering dress, checked her hair and placed their favourite wine glasses on the table. Then she glanced through the food dispenser menu to see what she should suggest for dinner. She was still looking through the menu when she heard him key in his number. He bounced in, his usual energetic self, and joked, ‘Just a simple snack in the café tonight then?’ He smiled as he walked straight to the shower, stripped and stepped in. Kessia took a large bath sheet and waited for him to finish. As soon as he did, she wrapped him in the towel and began to pad him dry. Then she kissed his shoulders and ran her fingers over the strange row of moles that ran down his spine. Running right from his hairline to his waist, they were short brown knobs equidistant from each other. He had been embarrassed the first time she noticed them but the months since then had built mutual respect and confidence. He took her in his arms, kissed her and said, ‘Go on – tell me! Tell me what it is you’re planning. I can tell you’re plotting something!’

She took a deep breath, felt her heart begin to pound and said as quickly as she could: ‘I’ve applied to leave the hormone programme and conceive our baby.’

There was a stunned silence and then, ‘What in the universe are you talking about?’

‘I’m going to come off the HPT,’ she said, but with less confidence, as she looked into his eyes, which seemed even greener than ever.

His response was something of an explosion: ‘Nobody in their right mind these days gets pregnant. We’ll use your egg if you like but leave me right out of this! Who in their right mind would want to carry their own baby, let alone one with my genes!’ and so on, culminating in, ‘Oh hell! When did you apply? Don’t tell me it’s happened already?’

Tearful, Kessia sat down and muttered, ‘Only today, so nothing’s happened yet. Why do you talk to me as if I’m stupid? I work in the repro business, I handle requests, examine the genetic details, witness the pathetic searches for perfection. I want my own child because I can’t think of a child I’d love more than one of my own that is yours too!’

Mercor sat quietly for a few moments, his head down. ‘I’m sorry,’ he said. ‘This is all my fault. I should have told you before. I’ll show you why we can’t do this. Will you come with me to meet my father? I’ll organise the security passes straight away and we’ll go tomorrow.’ He didn’t wait for her reply but, still wrapped in the towel, took his communicator from out of the pile of clothes left on the floor and started to speak into it.

Kessia already knew that he regularly visited his father who lived and worked in Avansor: an isolated, high security Tower about two hundred kilometres away for which she, Kessia, did not have access. Here the world's most highly respected space scientists lived, though exactly what they did was a mystery to most people. His mother had also worked there but she was killed years before in a freak accident whilst on a routine Earth-Moon shuttle.

Mercor had never spoken of any other family members and she had not probed further. She sensed there was something else, something he was not ready to share with her. Now, listening to his communications with the official pass office, the transport office and his father, she learnt a little more. The father's name was unusual, Gel Fidor. His status had recently been downgraded from security level one to security level two which meant he was now able to receive guests beyond his son and immediate work colleagues if all security measures were met. Mercor would fly himself there with Kessia, arriving at 10 and leaving at 17 hours. Passing through security, both would give the secrecy pledge and then would be allowed to visit any parts of the centre below number one security if supervised by Gel himself. When Mercor had finished the arrangements, he turned to her with an embarrassed smile and apologised for his hasty actions. 'I can't explain,' he said. 'You have to see for yourself.'

It was a strange and tense evening that followed, as if a wall of secrets stood between them; so, after a restless night, Kessia was happy and excited when the new day came. She had never before been in Mercor's work transport and had only ever flown twice before so the journey was breathtaking. Leaving the city towers behind them they passed large tracts of cultivated land, rivers and even some pockets of forest before they rose even higher to cross the mountain range. Finally they landed on the roofadrome of Avansor.

By the security booth a short man in a hat pulled right down to his eyes was waiting for them. He embraced his son and then turned to Kessia with a warm smile. She had a slight shock of recognition – he had the same green eyes she loved in Mercor, but accentuated by an amber lustre in his complexion. His voice had a faint trace of a foreign accent as he greeted her and shook her hand warmly. She was surprised by the unusual texture of his hand.

Passing the security portal, the three took the lift to level sixty nine and were soon in his apartment which was obviously his place of work too. There were several screens and various other technical devices Kessia could not name. Surprisingly, there were also several old-fashioned writing tools on the desk and she noticed an open book with handwritten mathematical formulae of amazing complexity. He noticed her surprise. 'My hobby,' he explained, 'to keep the old brain working.'

'Don't be afraid to take your hat off,' Mercor said to his father as he helped Kessia take off her coat. The older man answered in his own language – an astonishing sound unlike any language she had previously heard.

'She has to know,' replied his son, but he gripped Kessia's hand tighter as if to warn her. When the hat came off, she could see why. Mercor had very sparse hair and eyebrows but this man had none at all: instead, from his prominent nose right over his head was what can only be described as a bony crest. The amber tinge of his complexion gave way to a golden brown colour on the crest. Kessia felt her cheeks burn as she tried to control her reactions and stay polite. Mercor tried to make a joke of the situation by saying, 'I only have little spines down my back but he has the full sized ones!' Gel obviously felt his son was being rather insensitive and offered her a seat and a strong drink. She accepted, deciding it was better to be transparent, to agree that she had been shocked. Gradually, as she sat and sipped her drink, the explanations came.

Gel had been still quite a young man when he first transferred to Avansor from the Jupiter project on Europa. He was part of a team whose brief was to find quicker, more efficient ways of enabling space travel; he worked alongside another team that was searching for suitable planets – places that could relieve an over-large population that had practically exhausted available resources, a problem just as pressing on his own planet as it was on Earth.

He had volunteered to be one of the first "aliens" to work on Earth and never regretted this choice. After that bleak moon where he had worked for eleven months and the preceding journey of many years through space, Avansor was paradise indeed. Not only did the tower block have all the necessary amenities and leisure facilities but it was even surrounded by acres of beautiful parkland. He had no need or wish to go anywhere else, especially after he met Hallia. They decided to have a child without using the customary in-vitro procedure because they feared they would not get clearance from the authorities and it would be better to claim they had not realised it could happen between dissimilar humanoids. When the embryo was shown to be healthy, the authorities did not express disapproval but welcomed it as a scientific step forward. The child, Mercor, was at first a level one secret, a highly valuable individual, mixing only with other Avansor children, but security relaxed as he grew into a "normal" young man with excellent social skills. Eventually he was reclassified and allowed to travel beyond Avansor on a level two secrecy contract. By that time he was by no means the only "inter" but he was the first. Though Hallia's death had initially devastated the little family, Gel now showed no sign of self-pity. He was, he insisted, privileged to have known two completely different worlds and to have a son that linked them.

After the explanations came the tour of the Avansor centre and then a meal from Gel's food dispenser that had been personalised to include dishes from his own planet. 'Not exactly the same of course,' he said. 'They haven't yet engineered the grains exactly right but it gives an idea.' There was so much to explain, so much to share, that all three were sorry when 1700 hours arrived and it was time to part. 'Perhaps security will be lowered further and you'll be able to visit us soon?' Kessia suggested, as the final goodbyes were said.

The sun being low in the sky, flying conditions were not easy and Kessia did not want to start any emotional outbursts while Mercor was at the controls. She sat back, still a little dazed, and turned over in her mind all she had learnt and all that had happened as she gazed under her feet at the beautiful landscape below her. Suddenly the world seemed larger in some way, as if her outlook had widened from global to universal. When they were safely landed, she breathed a sigh, took his hand, returned the smile he gave, looked straight into his twinkling green eyes and said, 'Now I want *your* baby even more!'

Haze

by K S Dearsley

Spring was always the hardest time: the air was laden with guilt. Arno breathed it in with the smell of sap rising. Spring was reddening the tips of the dogwood and swelling the ends of twigs with its promise. Arno felt its pull, sweet and sad, a time of things passing. He glanced towards the house. Its veranda remained empty. He had bought the place where the mountains met the desert because he had thought it would remind Melian of Lyria. Thought of the lavender planet made him glance at the sky in the direction where he believed the planet ought to be. He went indoors.

The sound of the news holo drew Arno through to the lounge. Melian was standing in the middle of holo images of Elector Gogard pushing his way into counsel chambers through rival bands of protesters. Those draped in varying shades of lavender and violet were as muscular and vocal as the grey-clad followers of the Sanctified Path. Melian's eyes glittered and his-her cheeks were flushed as if she-he was feeling spring after all. Then Arno noticed that the hermaphrodite's elegant fingers were crushed into fists.

'We have to go to the capital.'

Melian's contralto could make "hello" sound like opera. Now it raised goose-pimples on Arno's forearms. She-he swept a gesture through the holo image of Intercessor Chell of the Sanctified Path. Arno had often felt like doing the same to the real man. His lip automatically twisted, but Melian shook his-her head.

'In this, he and I agree.'

As Arno concentrated on the news interview, for a moment the holo of the intercessor was overlaid on Melian's features. The sensation was disturbing. Chell smiled at the interviewer. He could have been a bank manager turning down a loan application.

'See what contact with the decadent society of Lyria has already done?' The holo followed his gaze to the lavender-clad protesters. Arno snorted.

'Wait,' Melian said.

'If Government agrees to Elector Gogard's demands for free trade with the planet, Earth would become ever more tainted... '

Arno exploded. 'Free trade! Are they mad?'

Melian rolled his-her eyes, silencing him.

The interviewer put another question. 'And what of Lyrian claims that we're endangering their planet's ecosystem?'

'Irrelevant.'

Arno wanted to take a wet dishcloth to the intercessor's smile.

Chell followed the elector into the counsel chamber and Arno cut the transmission.

'You see?' Melian said.

'I see the same bigoted greedy fools we've had to deal with ever since we came back.' Arno sighed. 'Okay. We'll go to the talks.'

'Thank you.' Melian put his-her hand on Arno's arm and Arno covered it with his own.

'I could go on my own,' Arno said and immediately had a flashback of Lyria; the naked androgynous bodies of people swaying in the quickening breeze. He had thought it some kind of ritual greeting of his ship, not realising that the lavender aura, that swirled in the air forming patterns he had been able to see even in orbit, was not clinging to their exposed bodies but emanating from them. How could he leave Melian with spring waking?

'The closed minds of the sanctified ones do not hurt me,' Melian said. 'I came here to learn and teach.'

'I'd hoped you'd come to share life with me as well.' Arno felt guilty even as he said it. 'You gave up everything. Why can't these "sanctified" ones see that? Everything.'

'I might never have borne fruit if I'd stayed on Lyria either. Not all of us do.' She-he put his-her arm around Arno's shoulders. It was not depriving the Lyrian of offspring that caused his guilt but the fact that he was glad of it.

There was plenty of time for reflection during their journey to the capital despite frequent recognition by their fellow passers on the super-track. Arno had suggested hiring a personal flier but Melian had rejected the idea.

'How are we to tell what the people think if we do not go among them?'

Arno had acquiesced. If Melian was prepared to put up with the irritation of Earth's dirt-laden air, he could tolerate people staring at the "hero of the Lyrian mission". Lyria had been a hazy arc wrapped in gauze through the window of the ship as he had begun his descent. Only the merest tremble in his breathe as he had reported on his ship's status had revealed his excitement. For the full length of the landing procedures Arno had also thought of himself as the hero of the Lyria mission, then he had stepped onto the planet. Pre-mature Lyrians had approached. He had turned to follow what he thought was their awe-struck gaze and seen it, the great rent his ship had torn in the violet swirls. Hero? Mass murderer, and yet they had treated him with courtesy and compassion. Maybe it was this that caused such disbelief. If a Lyrian had committed such an atrocity on Earth, there would have been calls to wipe out all of their kind. How could Arno have been forgiven if the violet dust was indeed the catalyst for Lyrian reproduction?

As if catching his thoughts, Melian said: 'We will make them understand.'

Arno shook his head. 'It's not in their interest to.'

Melian smiled at something beyond his shoulder and Arno sighed: another one! A saucer-eyed boy sidled up to his seat and held out a marker pad.

'Can I have your print please?' He spoke to Arno, but his stare was for Melian.

Arno handed the pad back to him.

The boy hesitated. 'Are you male or female?' He finally blurted at Melian.

'Don't you use the ed-interface?' Arno said.

The boy nodded. 'But the news holos say Lyrians tell us their planet's covered in baby dust to keep us out.'

Melian tried to hide a grin. 'Well, now you have seen me. What do you think?'

'I think you're beautiful.' The words tumbled out and the boy made a dash back to his seat.

'Baby dust!' Arno shook his head, but the boy was right about one thing: Melian was beautiful. His-her wheat-coloured hair had a sheen and his-her long limbs had recovered their fluid grace. The Lyrian had been growing sere little by little. Arno had not realised it until now. He gulped down panic and tried to concentrate on their destination.

They almost made it up the steps to the counsel chamber unnoticed. Melian's height and gliding grace should have caught people's gaze anywhere, particularly here, where so many had gathered with opinions on his-her kind, but they arrived as Intercessor Chell emerged and the violet-clad protesters were too busy chanting against him and his followers to see anything else. A shriek warned Arno and Melian that they had been spotted. There was an immediate cloud of lavender-hued chiffon as the "haze" users began waving their arms in an imitation of the quickening.

'There we see the cause of this orgiastic filth that's degrading Earth society!' Intercessor Chell's voice was muffled by the cloth he bundled in front of his mouth and nose.

The tilt of Melian's head and his-her half smile warned Arno. He grabbed the Lyrian's arm before she-he could turn back to speak to the Intercessor.

'Not now. Let's see how the land lies first.'

Inside, they found the discussions were in recess. Groups of delegates stood in knots or mingled, flowing between one and another, forming and reforming alliances and obligations like grains of sand swirled in a pail of water. Melian and Arno drifted among them. Whenever the Lyrian appeared in public people assumed that Arno would be at his-her side, and did not look for him elsewhere. It made it easy for him to wander away and eavesdrop. He lingered by a table laden with soft drinks and energy bites where two delegates were discussing the morning's proceedings while hesitating over the platters.

'Come on, Jameson, download. I know you've had a ship orbiting Lyria for the past cycle. What is it? Black-market Lyrian metals?' said one around a mouthful of something pink.

The other delegate continued loading his plate.

'Haze then.'

'You'll see.' Arno caught the look that passed between the delegate and Elector Gogard. Put Arno and the elector side by side and no one would be in any doubt that it was Gogard who was the hero. Yet there was something in his smile, which never penetrated beyond skin depth, that made Arno uneasy. Seeing that smile shared with the trade delegate gave his uneasiness a sour taste. The elector must have felt Arno's look. His gaze shifted to the former astro-explorer, and the insincere smile grew wider as he approached with hand outstretched.

'So, our "hero" has come to keep an eye on us.'

Arno would have ignored the hand, but Melian glided away from a group of the curious and came to stand beside him.

'Melian.' Elector Gogard hesitated then bowed. Humans could still only see things as either-or. Even the elector felt awkward in face of and-both.

'You didn't think we would miss such important discussions, surely.' Arno gave the elector's hand a firm shake, and was gratified to see Gogard wince.

'The country air suits you, Melian, you're blooming. Naturally, since your retirement from public life... no one believed you would want to come, otherwise I would have ensured that you and your... er... partner were invited.'

Arno glanced at Melian to see if she-he felt the sting of the compliment. His-her smile remained serene. She-he shook his-her head at Arno's anxious expression. 'The time is long past,' she-he said. Yet Arno could still smell spring.

A ripple of muttering spread from the doorway.

'Ah, the intercessor returns. Time, I think, to find our seats again.' Gogard signalled a steward. 'Make sure our guests have places on the dais.'

Where they would be in full view, honoured guests or exhibits. Arno did not like it, but there was no time to argue. Intercessor Chell swept past, a trail of grey acolytes in his wake creating eddies of disturbance that started a flow of delegates back into the counsel chamber. They took their places. As Elector Gogard recapped on the meeting so far, Arno's gaze skimmed over the audience. When Arno had returned to Earth with Melian, the looks that she-he drew might have been full of fear or respect but there was always awe as well, even on the faces of the followers of the Sanctified Path. Arno searched for it now and in many faces it was missing. The trade delegates, in particular, tended to whisper and grin as if she-he was a party doll. Arno tried to breathe in the remembered calm of Lyria. Melian sat at his side with hands folded in his-her lap as if listening to music that no one else could hear.

'So, there it is. For fifteen years we've respected the Lyrian restrictions on trade with the planet. We've done everything they've asked – and now they're claiming that we're threatening the future of their species.' Before Gogard could sit down there were shouts from the floor.

'How are we supposed to make a living?'

'They just want to push the prices up.'

Intercessor Chell rapped his fist on the arm of his chair. 'Leave them to their corruption and foul practices. Their metals are bought at too high a price. All you need to do is step outside to see how their unholy ways are tainting our youth. It's Earth's future that's at risk here, not Lyria's. There are those among you... ' He pointed accusingly and the audience squirmed. '...who trade in their filth...'

'And why not?' Gogard interrupted without raising his voice. The intercessor's shock gave him the silence he needed. The elector produced a phial from his pocket. 'I have here a sample of this so-called quickening catalyst, known to our lavender-dressed users as "haze".'

Arno was half out of his seat. Melian took his hand. The Lyrian's eyes glittered and she-he sighed. Arno had seen that hunger before and it was not on the faces of the users outside.

Intercessor Chell sat further back in his chair as if simply being close to the dust could pollute him.

'Don't worry, Intercessor,' Gogard said, shaking the phial. 'The container's sealed, and even if it wasn't there's nothing to fear. I've had the dust analysed, and you know what? Our poor deluded youths have been breathing in nothing more harmful than amino acids and traces of minerals. Reproductive catalyst? Lyrian sweat.' He sat back enjoying the uproar.

'Liar! Tricks!' Someone threw a glass at Melian and the meeting erupted. Arno held his breath, ready to get between Melian and the crowd.

'They've robbed us!'

'Liar!'

Melian's eyes remained fixed on the phial of dust.

Gogard rose once more. 'Not liars – mistaken, perhaps. The Lyrians sincerely believe that dust like that in this phial is an essential part of their reproductive process – I'm sure once we enlighten them, they'll remove all their restrictions.'

'And how do you propose to do that?' Arno was on his feet. 'With battle-liners and strike teams?'

There was a low rumble from the audience that could have been a growl of consent.

'I'm sure that won't be necessary.' Gogard's tone was fatherly, but he brandished the phial as if it was a trophy. 'No, the Lyrians will see sense especially with missionaries from the Sanctified Path to persuade them of their mistake.'

Intercessor Chell's tirade against the politician's outrage stopped mid-flow. Elector Gogard was offering him a chance to convert the population of a whole planet – to his glory or God's, it was all the same – and in the process avert a war. Earth would probably bow down and adore him too. Except that there could be no war. The Lyrians had no missiles and could not launch them if they did – not without destroying the very thing they were trying to protect. The first attack by Earth would disrupt the weather patterns, burn the dust... It might take a generation, but then Earth, without directly killing one Lyrian or setting foot on the planet, would have an empty world to take over. Greed and prejudice; both were unknown on Lyria, where the catalyst parent might have come from a few feet away or the other side of the planet. There were no bloodlines or races. All Lyrians were valued equally, for who could say with certainty from whose heritage they sprang? Arno glared at the faces around him, seeing only prejudice and contempt.

'How can you believe him?' he demanded.

'Ah, Arno speaks, the "hero of Lyria" with his alien lover. If you want proof, it sits right there.' Gogard pointed at Melian, who sat with eyes half-closed and his-her breath coming rapidly. 'In all the years it's lived here, has there been even a hint of it quickening?'

Arno felt his own breath becoming more rapid. He wanted to mash the elector's face against the table. He turned helplessly to Melian. His-her eyes met Arno's. There was no other way.

'We have no one's word for this except Elector Gogard's. How can we even be sure that it's Lyrian dust in that tube?'

'Is that your best argument?' Gogard held the phial up to the light so that the contents seemed to glow.

'There's only one way we can all be sure: give the dust to Intercessor Chell and let him have it tested.'

'Yes.' The intercessor's face was exultant. His fingers were already twitching to hold the phial as he approached the elector.

Arno turned to Melian and she-he nodded.

'Ridiculous! The intercessor has a vested interest.'

'And you don't? Proof should be left to those who are only interested in the truth and not financial gain.' Arno was aware of an angry swell of conflicting noise from the supporters of both groups. Chairs were being scraped back and scuffles breaking out. 'He has no right to that dust. If it is real, he stole it. How can you trust the fate of two planets to a thief?' Arno gave the pot another stir, holding his hand out to Melian, who rose as if dazzled by the glow from the dust.

'Only the pure can do God's work!' Intercessor Chell made a grab for the phial. Elector Gogard flung his arm back to keep it from reach. The phial slipped and his fingers tightened around it. There was a crunch as Arno stepped forward and wrapped his fist around Gogard's, pressing it against the shards of glass. Gogard struggled to release his hand and Arno let go so that the elector's arm swept up in an arc scattering a trail of lavender dust that leaked between his fingers. Intercessor Chell snatched up his handkerchief, covered his face and fell back, but Arno was only dimly aware of the chaos in the rest of the room. His skin tingled where the dust touched him. Through a blur of tears he watched Melian let his-her robe fall to the floor and enter the cloud of lavender. She-he seemed almost to float in it, his-her arms and body as sinuous as plants in a slow-flowing river.

'Melian,' Arno whispered the name, knowing that she-he would not hear him now.

'Obscene! Obscene!' Intercessor Chell's cry brought the rest of the room to a halt. Then even he fell quiet, mesmerised by the slow, graceful dance of the quickening. At first Arno was not sure that he was actually seeing the darker violet hue and that it was not merely an effect of the light, but then Melian's swirling movements made it certain. Arno led him-her by the fingertips through the packed counsel chamber and outside where the spring winds joined Melian in his-her dance and took his-her dust higher and higher, hazier and hazier.

The haze users, the followers of the Sanctified Path, the news holo teams and the curious – all saw and all were held by the quiet ecstasy of Melian's quickening.

'Let any of them try to deny it now.'

Melian gave no sign of being aware of any of it. The Lyrian's movements were gradually slowing as the moment Arno had dreaded for so long began to pass. He watched, clutching the robe she-he had discarded, ready to wrap the Lyrian in it as if it was a shield of love. At last Melian's arms dropped to his-her sides. She-he shivered and took a deep breath, before raising his-her head and seeing Arno. He could say nothing.

She-he stroked his face. 'All things pass.'

Arno draped the robe around Melian and he guided him-her away.

They went back to the desert and let the vibrations that Melian's quickening had triggered ripple around the planet – faster even than the Lyrian's wind-borne dust. News holos of his-her dance of life were repeated, it seemed on the hour, for days afterwards. Arno recorded them, but could not watch: perhaps one day he would find release in the pain of seeing it again. Extremists and politicians of all shades demanded access to them; the hero of Lyria had become indispensable in devising the new accord between the lavender planet and Earth – and then came the polite enquiries after Melian.

'Blooming,' Gogard had said in the counsel chamber, and for a while she-he was. There had always been something of the tall stately flower about him-her.

Intercessor Chell came to their aid. 'If I did not believe what my eyes saw, I would have to believe what my heart felt when...'

When Melian had given his-her life. At least the intercessor could now understand Arno's guilt. Melian would have none of it, and Arno could never be quite sure exactly where the real sacrifice had been: avoiding the quickening or embracing it. Either way, Melian's actions had been driven by love for him and for Lyria, but mostly for him. Looking at the rosy-cheeked fruit of the quickening, Arno could not doubt it. As Melian had begun to brown and wither, his-her hair crinkling and breaking like strands of old leaves and his-her movements becoming jerky as his-her limbs dried to old stalks, the new-born, at first as delicate as a lacewing, had wrapped tendrils of affection around Arno's heart. It did not matter that Arno was not the fruit's progenitor. She-he was Melian's gift to him.

'Don't grieve,' Melian had said, his-her voice like the rustle of dry grass. 'She-he will love as I have loved.'

Arno had tried to promise him-her that he would take the fruit to see Lyria, that he would protect it, even that he would do as Melian asked and not grieve, but no words had come. Melian had smiled.

It was the same smile Arno saw now on the face of his-her offspring. They stood hand in hand and watched as the wind took the sere remains and scattered them across the desert while the intercessor read the service. Melian had always thought the words the most beautiful of all the human rituals: ashes to ashes, dust to dust.

About Earlyworks Press Genre Challenges

This book is the result of the latest Earlyworks Press 'Genre Challenge'. The challenges are run at the instigation of members of our writers' forum or of the wider circle of writers who work with us. They are designed to investigate questions about different kinds of writing and they have never failed to produce a crop of interesting and enjoyable stories.

In 2006 **The High Fantasy Challenge** asked whether there was any mileage left in tales of elves and wizards. It turned out that there was, and to prove it, the best of the entries were published in **The Sleepless Sands** anthology.

The first **Science Fiction Challenge**, which ran in 2007, was a search for sci-fi writing 'with real humans', as opposed to interchangeable characters in silver suits serving to make a point. The resulting anthology, **The Road Unravelled** has a remarkable set of characters grappling with current issues in real-world science and technology.

In 2008, the **Gender Genre Challenge** sought evidence of differences in male and female writing styles. The top ten stories from this one were published on the Earlyworks Press website (look for the page called Gender Genre Short Story Competition). By then, our poets were feeling left out so we also ran the **Rhymers' Competition**, to see what contemporary writers would make of what many see as an old fashioned way of writing poetry. (Look for the page called Rhymers' Poetry Competition Winners).

In 2009, the illustrations came first as our artists put forward a collection of paintings and photos designed to encourage new takes on old tales. The result was the **Old Magic in a New Age** anthology.

In 2010, the **Memoir and Journalism Challenge** was set to find the issues of the 20th century that were going to make history from a literary point of view. At the time of writing (spring 2012) we are preparing an illustrated anthology of the best entries.

In 2011, we returned to science fiction when club member David Dennis marked the development of the James Webb telescope, and the resultant speculation about the search for alien intelligence, by setting a challenge he called **Alien Co-Operation**. Could we meet and communicate with races from other planets? What issues should we be thinking about to facilitate successful interplanetary relations?

The stories in **Telescoping Time** are our favourites from the entries offering answers – or further questions to consider.

Telescoping Time marks a turning point for us because it is the first of the competition anthologies to be launched in ebook form. The previous anthologies currently exist only on paper but ebook publication of a 'Best of...' set from previous competitions and challenges is planned for later this year (2012). Keep an eye on the **Publications Page** at Earlyworks Press if you'd like a copy when it comes out.

If you have an idea for a new genre challenge, drop us an email and let us know. If you'd like to see your own work in our future anthologies, please visit the **Competitions Page** at Earlyworks Press for details of the current competitions and challenges.

The internationally popular short story, poetry and flash fiction competitions run every year, and the Genre Challenges from time to time. All offer cash prizes and publication opportunities.

www.earlyworkspress.co.uk

The book of the High Fantasy Challenge

"Please, no more magic sword romps," they say. "Elves, dwarves and rustic spirits have had their day. High fantasy has scraped the barrel clean, there is no more."

"To win this competition, prove them wrong," we said, "Send us a new fantasy story or poem that feels as magical as one of the old favourites, but isn't just a rehash."

This book celebrates the work of those who we feel answered the challenge with heroic success.

First among them is R D Gardner's *The Binding of the Sleepless Sands*. The elements of the story are traditional, and true to their mythic form; the story is well crafted and original. The plot is excruciatingly applicable to the political, social and psychological dilemmas we face today. The ending is unexpected, and the terrible dilemma it creates will follow you around for a long time.

As for poetry, Gardner's *Wizardry and Second-Hand Romance* is a clear demonstration of the problem this competition set out to investigate – why some people think high fantasy has outstayed its welcome – but Steve Mann's *...and here he is, himself...* gives us the solution: we see the modern seeker tentatively approaching a mythic hero, and coming back with something new. And Mann's *Kizmet* closes the collection on the note all high fantasy should end with – doubt, paradox and possibility.

The range of poems, stories and artwork in between is enormous. Traditional, modern, comic, romantic and deadly – but every one adds something to the recipe book. Enjoy them and take heart – the sun is not yet setting on high fantasy!

Kay Green, August 2006

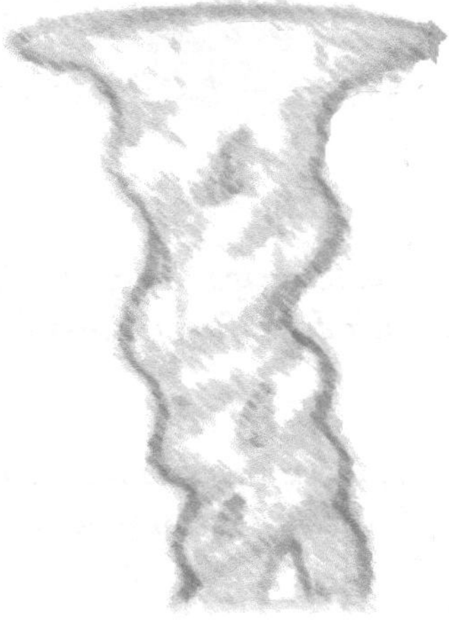

The Dragon Tower sketch by Katy Jones

Other illustrations by Nikola Temkov, Jenna Whyte and Suryan Philip

The Book of the First Earlyworks Press Science Fiction Challenge

'We're looking for stories that are a credible picture of where we might be heading – or where we could end up if... Stories should conform to the sci-fi 'What if...?' genre, that is, they should be predictions backed by credible if not actual science.

But the science must stay in the background. We want stories you can read without having an MSc! And they must have real, in depth characters, not just manikins to drive the space ships.

There are lists of 'over-used sci-fi plots' going around the web. Can you make one of these plots worth visiting again, or do you have a truly original idea?'

That was the challenge, and this book is the authors' answer to it. They have given us theories about god, genetics, mortality and human responsibility. They have asked what can and cannot be done with computers, robots and AI, and what it is that makes us human.

The result is some startling predictions that raise some mind-melting questions. Enjoy them, think on them, and sleep if you dare!

Here are some extracts…

From **Chucking Out Time** by R D Gardner

'Matt, what would I have to do?'

'Have another beer, and shut your eyes: this has to go in your spinal cord.'

'Er, Matt, how much have you had?'

'Relax, I've never impaled a rat yet.'

The needle went into the back of my neck.

I don't remember to this day what we did then, or how I got home: the students next door assured me I came home at sunrise, singing:

Never get bombed with a boffin,
you never know where it might end,
Don't get laboratory ratted,
and do what you didn't intend...

From **Experimental Use of the Drug Axenphenicol Lithium Sulphate in Forensic Criminology** by David Dennis

Strands of seaweed stroked my face, like the hair of some mermaid or lost maiden. I tried to catch them in the vain hope that they were anchored to some rock which might help me save myself. There was a roaring in my ears. When I came up for air I saw the shining sea wall and on it was some writing in white foaming letters, tall and broad: 'DID DADDY TOUCH YOU?' it said.

Then someone dived in and rescued me.

From **Going Away** by Vanessa Lafaye

On the drive to the Facility, Julianne and James revisited their favourite moments from the past on the handheld viewer. They were conspiring together, both focused on the happy images of their miniature selves being replayed in the back seat of the taxi…

'How long?' he asked. She closed and opened her eyes to view her Life Clock and said flatly, '20 minutes.' He stroked her hand, hoping that his touch would register even if she was almost beyond the reach of his voice.

From **Transcript** by Clive Gilson

'Shit.'

The Boss leans forward.

'Run silent!'

Lights shift to red. Unlike ancient submariners, silent running means that all external scans and counter-measures are killed. Sound is immaterial. We exist within our cloak, blind, with our ears cocked for the sound of heavy footfalls over our shoulder.

'Destroyer peeling off and dropping in behind us,' Dewey explains. 'Thing is, we don't know if it's seen us or if it's routine. They drop back in rotation every couple of hours to see if anyone is following. Standard defensive tactics.'

I struggle to make my mouth work, swallowing to force the glands in my mouth to produce saliva. My heart is thumping in my chest. 'How do we know…'

'If you see a very bright white light then you're dead.' He laughs out loud. 'Only way to know for sure. If you're still looking at me in ten minutes then chances are they're none the wiser. Tick-tock, tick-tock.' The bastard is grinning like a Cheshire Cat.

From **Mission Statement** by Peter Caunt

The return into normal space came with a heavy jolt, and a striking pain down his left side. At least it would have been pain if he had been human. The damage sensors had simply registered a severe fault condition on the port engine intakes, but he liked to think of it as pain.

From **Zingibers** by Kim Green

Nervous. Excited. Satisfied. Outraged. These were some reactions to the new enclosure of The Earth Zoo… Everyone agreed though, that the new enclosure was *important*, and could not be dismissed from the mind easily by anyone who cared for the future of the Earth.

From **Hippo with Three Eyes** by Martin Pevsner

Hey, man. Need any more of that? Need anything at all? I whip round, see that I'm being watched. He's a mean-looking bloke, weasel face, greasy brown hair centre-parted, thin lips, sharp nose. He's smiling at me knowingly. He's seen me necking the pill. I say nothing, looking him over. I register his lasertat, an *XXX*, on his neck. It's the symbol of the Pig klan, a large Bandon crew, not to be messed with.

Where you from, Blud? he asks. I tell him. *You lads are cool. Well known fact, the Hiiippos from Kroyden are the hardest village klan. I'd be honoured to do some business with you.*

From **An Invisible Rose** by Catherine Edmunds

Kevin shuffled a pile of plasma records on Rachel's desk and patted her head, looking disconcerted when his hand fell straight through her scalp.

'Urrgh,' he muttered, turning away blushing.

'Sorry Kev, you were saying?'

…Kevin spun round and marched away, tripping over a waste-plasma bin. Rachel watched the mechanised safety rope swing into action, lassoing his wrist to prevent him falling, but pulling his arm out of its socket in the process. A medic-droid dropped down from the ceiling and whacked Kevin on the shoulder, fixing the problem with startling efficiency.

From **The Beautiful Mind of Samuel Bland Arnold** by David Dennis

I will tell you why I cannot reveal my love for Patty. There is only one phrase for it: fear of rejection. How can you continue to command a ship this size when your deputy has told you she does not reciprocate your love and yet you are both immortal? You would have to live with your shame and embarrassment forever. ... If I were wrong it would stain my memory with ugliness and breach the Arcado Doctrine.

From **The Extinction Paradox** by Kenneth Shand

'So what's your future, Gorn?' Kayib was getting aggressive.

'I'll operate the Faith Stream a while longer, maybe get promoted, have lots of little Gorns…'

'Let me stop you right there.'

'I've seen them. All my flame haired little Gorn-alikes.'

'You mean you get them all to look like you?'

'Every one of them.'

'That's so vain it's despicable.'

'Well I'm the perfect model after all.'

'And you've seen them?'

'On screen I have, and I've had them dance around as avatars.'

'Despicable, I tell you.'

'Aleph help us all.'

From **Catherine and the God Market** by Sheila Adamson

On Tuesday night Catherine answered the doorbell to find two aliens outside. It took her a while to work out how to react to that.

'Hallo!' said the alien on the left. 'Can we interest you in a message of hope and gladness?'

'Uh?' she said.

The alien smiled brightly. At least, she thought it was smiling. It had a huge lipless mouth, which it was stretching widely; and huge owl eyes which it was blinking enthusiastically. It also had three arms, three legs and rather scaly grey skin. Presumably in an attempt to blend in, it was wearing a dark business suit. 'Are you happy?' it enquired.

'Em…'

'Truly happy?'

Catherine felt herself edging backwards. Strangers weren't supposed to ask you questions like that. Of course she wasn't happy. What business was it of anyone else's, human or not?

'We'd like to tell you about true happiness,' said the second, smaller alien.

'And eternal life.'

'May we come in?'

The Myth and Legend Challenge

Standing stones and churches, trees and totems, fairytale creatures; dragons, princes, gods, ghosts and elementals from Europe and beyond... We asked our writers and illustrators to dig deep, find the mythic and magical figures that spoke to them, and show us why they have survived into the New Age.

The result is a fabulous collection of stories and artwork. Some of the motifs are familiar and faithful, others have evolved as the world has changed. So if modern life leaves you hungry, enter these pages and find out which eternal classics still speak your personal magical language.

Here are some extracts...

From **Nature's Banquet** by Jonathan Pinnock

You can smell it in the air, can't you? Blossom in the trees, dew on the meadow grass and the pungent whiff of steamy cowpats. Spring, and the world has come out of hibernation. And God, isn't this a good place to be in the bright early morning? Just you and Bonzo and Nature. Christ knows, you needed to get away from everything in the City right now. Away from all that fakery and bullshit. This is the real deal...

From **The Ash Lady** by A.J. Humphrey

You think I can't see you sloping off into the night like that. I'm asleep, you presume, where I can't do any mischief. The house is quiet: my daughters at the ball, the servants enjoying a night of freedom. But you really should have thought about this more carefully, Sarah. How could a gilded coach with white stallions and footmen appear outside the walls and not attract my attention?

I'm always watching you, if only you knew it. I've watched you grow up, the girl who has everything. You're the prettiest girl in the city; that tongue of yours can silence me with a single word some days; and don't get me started on the size of the trust fund your father left. Next to you, my own two daughters are plain and slow. They have to make do with home-made dresses and their mother for a lady-in-waiting...

From **One. Two. Three.** by Bryan Martin

Once I have got to the place I don't mind taking my top stuff off. I just grab hold of the bottom of my jumper and T shirt all together and lift them up and pull my head out and that feels all right. It feels the way it should be. But I feel funny when I am taking my trousers and pants and socks off. I never really like that and I don't like the way I have to stand on one leg to do it. It feels too real. I wish I could just pull everything all off in one go and be standing there ready straight away. But there is no getting round it, really, when I do the thing...

From **Swan Heart** by Jess Richards

In this town the church is on the floor on top of the library. Hymns are sung above a graveyard of carefully hand picked books. My friend Nessi borrowed a dictionary of witches and faeries. Her mother was phoned by the head librarian who told her to fix a closer eye on her daughter. She didn't tell her she borrowed it for me. That I secretly asked her to help me find out about wings and why they grew on humans. We couldn't find the answer anyway.

Men demand to buy us girls a drink. We tell them no, they get angry and foul mouthed. We back down. When they've bought it they think we're theirs for the night and punch walls if we say no to that as well. Hands with skinned knuckles can be far too persuasive. I think we should all just start charging them money, make it more honest...

From **Pendine Remembered** by Sarah Thomasin

His elder sister waited for the tide.
She sulked. And, feeling robbed of precious time,
And forced to watch her brother dodge and hide
Among the rocks she'd told him not to climb,
Coating his shirt in dark, organic slime
That she'd be blamed for, called to him, and lied.

Her little brother never knew she lied:
His clever sister understood the tide,
Did algebra, and knew why slugs made slime -
He trusted her pronouncements every time.
She'd showed him starfish, taught him how to climb.
And what she said now made him want to hide...

From **Open Mic Apollo** by Thérèse Whitelock

As soon as the Sun God appeared on the dusty stage, my journalistic neutrality left the building. Before he sung a note I knew I was in trouble.

He was only a boy but he locked eyes with the jaded musos in that Camden pub and subjugated them. It had been one rough night, all bunny hopping power chords and tearful acoustic picking, so Apollo's brutal command provoked an expectant silence...

~~~
~~~